Elizabeth Barrett Browning, Richard H. Horne

Letters of Elizabeth Barrett Browning Addressed to Richard Hengist Horne

Vol. I

Elizabeth Barrett Browning, Richard H. Horne

Letters of Elizabeth Barrett Browning Addressed to Richard Hengist Horne
Vol. I

ISBN/EAN: 9783337016982

Printed in Europe, USA, Canada, Australia, Japan

Cover: Foto ©Raphael Reischuk / pixelio.de

More available books at **www.hansebooks.com**

LETTERS

OF

ELIZABETH BARRETT BROWNING

ADDRESSED TO

RICHARD HENGIST HORNE,

AUTHOR OF "ORION," "GREGORY VII.," "COSMO DE' MEDICI," ETC.

𝔚𝔦𝔱𝔥 𝔠𝔬𝔪𝔪𝔢𝔫𝔱𝔰 𝔬𝔫 𝔠𝔬𝔫𝔱𝔢𝔪𝔭𝔬𝔯𝔞𝔯𝔦𝔢𝔰.

EDITED BY

S. R. TOWNSHEND MAYER.

VOL. I.

LONDON:

RICHARD BENTLEY AND SON,

𝔓𝔲𝔟𝔩𝔦𝔰𝔥𝔢𝔯𝔰 𝔦𝔫 𝔒𝔯𝔡𝔦𝔫𝔞𝔯𝔶 𝔱𝔬 𝔥𝔢𝔯 𝔐𝔞𝔧𝔢𝔰𝔱𝔶 𝔱𝔥𝔢 𝔔𝔲𝔢𝔢𝔫.

1877.

Hazell, Watson, and Viney, Printers, London and Aylesbury.

PREFATORY NOTE.

MANY of the following letters are now published for the first time; the rest have appeared, after varying intervals, in the *Contemporary Review*, *Macmillan's*, and the *St. James's* Magazines, my task as editor being limited to their classification and rearrangement in chronological order for the present volumes. The connecting narrative is of course from the pen of Mr. Horne, who has interpolated no more than was necessary for elucidation—though had he extended his comments it would, I venture to think, have been ungrudgingly pardoned in an author who is one of the few remaining links between the period of Wordsworth and Shelley, and the risen and rising stars of the present day.

The spiritual strength of Miss Barrett's letters, combined with the modest self-estimate, and temporary forgetfulness of her dangerous state of health, which they evince, renders them unique. The struggle, not only for emancipation from solitude but for life itself, during which they were written, gives them psychological as well as literary value in the key they supply to her mind as expressed in her poems. It is, moreover, a curious fact that the correspondents had never met.

" Long absence from England, variety " of occupation, and bush life in Australia,

" added to motives of delicacy in the fear
"of intruding on unclosed wounds from the
" loss of such a spirit," says Mr. Horne,
will account for the delay in giving to
the world this mine of literary wealth—
a delay which would have been prolonged
but for the sudden discovery that many
of Miss Barrett's letters were beginning
to fade. "Her graphic lines," he continues, "were in several instances on
" the borders of the vanishing point."
Under these circumstances he asked
permission of his friend, Mr. Robert
Browning, for their publication, and
this (although Mr. Browning had never
seen the letters) was granted at once, in
terms which enhanced the favour as
much beyond our means to express as
it would be beyond his wish that we
should make the attempt.

I need only add that the "Recollections of Contemporaries," concluding Volume II., are entirely from the pen of Mr. Horne; and that we are greatly indebted to Mr. Richard Gowing for kindly permitting us to reprint—with slight alterations—from the pages of the *Gentleman's Magazine*, the two articles on "The Guild of Literature and Art."

.S. R. TOWNSHEND MAYER.

RICHMOND, SURREY,
November 21st, 1876.

CONTENTS OF VOL. I.

CORRIGENDA TO VOLUME I.

Page 4, line 8 from top, for "Lady Mary Wortley Montague" *read* "Lady Mary Wortley-Montagu"

,, 16, line 2 from bottom, "very few grand things" *dele* "few"

,, 21, line 1 at top, for "Miss Haydon" *read* "Mr. Haydon"

,, 27, note, last line, for "section in the *Post*" *read* "see Vol. II., p. 61, *et seq.*"

,, 30, line 4 from top, for "faults" *read* "fault"

,, 54, line 8 from top, for "for beauty" *read* "for the beauty"

,, 91, line 6 from bottom, for "Diety" *read* "Deity"

,, 101, last line, for "Leonard Schmitz" *read* "Leonhard Schmitz"

,, 151, top line, for "we went" *read* "she went"

,, 238, line 7 from top, for "found" *read* "fond"

,, 270, line 11 from top, for "orgy of fawns" *read* "orgy of fauns."

I.

Early Letters.

.

VOL. I.

I.

EARLY LETTERS.

Letter-writing a Lost Art—Celebrated Letter-writers—
Miss Mitford—Miss Elizabeth Barrett Barrett—First
Introduce Miss Barrett to the Public—The "Death-
Fetches"—Death of Miss Barrett's Brother—"Gregory
VII."—Tragic Influence—"Orion" Seedlings—Hoop-
ing-Cough—Miss Sedgwick's Book on America—The
Syncretics—The *Monthly Chronicle* and its Fate—
"The Seraphim" and other Poems—The Theatrical
Patent Monopolies — Petition against them—Miss
Barrett's Refusal to Sign—Portrait of Keats—"Orion"
—Miss Katherine Cockell—Beauty in Women—Shy-
ness—Recollections of Mary Russell Mitford—*Black-
wood*—My Visit to Three Mile Cross—Harriet Mar-
tineau — American Reviews of Tennyson—Robert
Montgomery.

A LADY with whom I have the honour
to be acquainted—the author of
some recently published volumes of true
poetry—is in the habit of excusing herself to her correspondents for the brevity

of her notes, on the ground that "letter-writing" is one of the lost arts. The present generation seems to have become "too fast" for it. Recalling to memory the celebrated letter-writers of a more leisurely literary period, — Madame de Sévigné, Madame de Staël, and Lady Mary Wortley Montague; and among men, the more highly finished and future-eyed letter-writers, such as Pope, Addison, Cowper, Horace Walpole, and others, one begins to see that there is much truth in the assertion. That the "loss" of the art is mainly attributable to an impatient sense of the loss of time will scarcely be denied, if we bring our view down to the nearer dates of the admirable letters of Robert Burns, of Southey, of Mary Russell Mitford, Leigh Hunt, Charles Dickens, Harriet Martineau, Sara Coleridge, and those of Elizabeth Barrett Browning, a portion of which are now first given to the world.

Putting mere fine talk out of court, and presupposing some brains, study, and experience, the art of letter-writing is just the art, so to speak, of being natural. In other words, it is not an *art* at all. Inasmuch as nobody comes to *read* with facility till a good deal of reading has been done; so in writing with facility, a considerable amount of previous writing is to be understood; and once taking this for granted, letter-writing, varying in character and excellence with the individual writer, is, in its highest forms of success, the natural and spontaneous outpouring of a well-stored intellect, a genial spirit, the wit and humour that comes unsought, and the *abandon* of soul and heart which arises from the full belief of addressing a congenial mind. Letters of this kind are the perfection of refined colloquiality. Those of Miss Mitford carried the carelessness of implicit confidence to an amusing extent, innumerable letters and notes from her having been written on any scraps of paper at hand, old envelopes turned inside out, and blank edges of newspapers, the outsides of many letters being frequently half covered with postscripts and after-thoughts. Those of Mrs. Browning had no external signs of this easy, off-hand carelessness, but *within* they were the perfection of confiding frankness, and the complete undisguised expression of the writer's thought and feeling upon every subject she touched.

It will be remembered that Miss Barrett, having been for years confined to her rooms, like an exotic plant in a green-house, being considered in constant danger of rapid decline, occupied herself in the arduous study of poetry, and in acquiring a knowledge of the Latin, Greek, and Hebrew languages. She was well acquainted with all the greatest authors of France and Italy, in the original, and she was a most assiduous reader of English literature, conversant equally with the earliest authors and the best of her own day. Her criticisms in the *Athenæum* are among the finest ever penned, discriminating and applauding all the power and beauty, lenient to errors and shortcomings, and rich with imaginative illustrations. That the same merits, united to a subtle instinct as to character, the more remarkable considering her years of seclusion, characterise her private letters, has hitherto only been known to the few who enjoyed her society, or ranked among her correspondents.

My first introduction to Miss Barrett

was by a note from Mrs. Orme, enclosing one from the young lady, containing a short poem, with the modest request to be frankly told whether it might be ranked as poetry or merely verse. As there could be no doubt in the recipient's mind on that point, the poem was forwarded to *Colburn's New Monthly*, edited at that time by Mr. Bulwer (afterwards the late Lord Lytton), where it duly appeared in the current number. The next manuscript sent to me was "The Dead Pan," and the poetess at once started on her bright and noble career.

It was thus my happiness to be instrumental in first introducing Miss E. B. Barrett to the literary world. In addition to this fact (to me a source of just pride), it must be remembered that I was many years her senior, that I had published several works, and had many literary engagements (with the whole of which she was fully acquainted), and that she knew of my varied experiences in foreign lands ; a combination which, acting upon her imagination in solitude, together with a most unexampled over-estimate of my services, evoked expressions of gratitude and deference, and which, with profound respect to her memory, I beg to disclaim. For the frequent reference, also, to my Tragedies and other works, let me ask the reader to grant me his pardon—the more necessary, if, as will be likely with so many readers of the present day, he has never read a line of them ; and it may strengthen my excuse for the inability to omit such passages, if I remind him that the books in question have been, for the most part, long out of print. Matters very clear in the letters as they stand would become misty and confused if I erased those passages.

The first of Miss Barrett's letters that I have been able to find refers to a contribution of mine, written at her request, to one of "Finden's Illustrated Annuals," edited by her friend Miss Mitford. I did not at all like these ornamental efflorescences of passing literature, as both ladies knew; the thing was done, nevertheless, being cast in the shape of a trilogy, founded on the German legend of the "Death-Fetches." I have never seen it since, nor has anybody else in all probability, for it shared the deserved fate of these annual gildings.

I.   "BEACON TERRACE, TORQUAY,
                      "Nov. 20th, 1839.

"MY DEAR SIR,—In passing to the immediate occasion of my troubling you with these lines, allow me to thank you —to join mine to the thanks of many —for the pleasure of admiration (surely not the least of the pleasures of this world) with which I have read your trilogy. It is so full of fine conception, that its brevity grows into a fault,—one would so willingly see it brought out into detail and consummation. But, even as it is, believe in my contentment—speaking for myself.

" The moonlight scene is exquisite, and there is (particularly distinguishable in that) a music of *broken cadences* which I have seldom observed out of Shakespeare. It is the Fetch of a great tragedy —for all the briefness.

" I should not have ventured to trouble you with opinions you might so easily take for granted, if it were not for another circumstance. Two months or more ago, you will remember asking me to send you a short poem by return of post, for a particular purpose. I was ill able to write at the time, but still worse able to endure the appearance of discourtesy towards you in such a trifle, and therefore I sent you two MSS. which I had by me, the shortest I had, but evidently too long to suit you. I did it just and only that you might not think me ill-natured; and the event having proved that uselessness to you otherwise, perhaps you would be kind enough to enclose them back to me—that is, if you can readily put your hand upon them. The 'Madrigal of Flowers' is one title, and the 'Cry of the Human' the other. I am afraid of involving you in some trouble of search for which you may well reproach me. So pray, if you cannot readily put your hand upon them, put the subject out of your head.

"Very sincerely yours,

"Elizabeth B. Barrett.

"To R. H. Horne,

"75, Gloucester Place, London."

The next letter alludes to a sad event —the drowning of Miss Barrett's brother, while on a boating excursion, almost before her eyes :—

II. [Postmark—Torquay, May 17th, 1840.]

" I shall be more at ease when I have thanked you, dear Mr. Horne, for your assurance of sympathy, which in its feeling and considerate expression, a few days since, touched me so nearly and deeply. Without it I should have written when I was able—I mean physically able—for, in the exhaustion consequent upon fever, I have been too weak to hold a pen. As to reluctancy of feeling, believe me that I must change more than illness or grief can change me, before it becomes a painful effort to communicate with one so very kind as you have been to me. Kindness and sympathy are not such common

things.   And as to the strangership—
why, a friend is proved by remaining
one in adversity.   You *began* to be one
in mine; and *for that reason*—a peculiarity which in separating you from the
class of ordinary friends removes you still
further from that of strangers—it is easier
for you to forget this, than for me.

" Besides the appreciated sympathy, I
have to acknowledge four proofs of your
remembrance, the seals of which lay un-
broken for a fortnight or more after their
removal here.   In one letter was something about ' neglect '—you told me never
to fancy a silence into a neglect.   Was I
likely to do it?   Was there any room
for even fancy to try?   That would be
still more surprising than the fact of
your making room for a thought of me
in the multitude of your occupations.

" You have been in the fields—I know

by the flowers—and found there, I suppose, between the flowers and the life
and dear Mrs. Orme, that pleasant dream
(for me!) about my going to London at
Easter. *I* never dreamt it. And while
you wrote, what a mournful contrary was
going on here! It was a heavy blow
(may God keep you from such! I knew
you would be sorry for me when you
heard). It was a heavy blow for all of us
—and I, being weak, you see, was struck
down as by a *bodily* blow, in a moment,
without having time for tears. I did not
think, indeed, to be better any more, but
I have quite rallied now—except as to
strength—and they say that on essential
points I shall not suffer permanently—
and this is a comfort to poor papa.

"But oh, Mr. Horne, God's will is so
high above humanity, that its goodness
and perfectness cannot be scanned at a

glance, and would be very terrible if it were not for His manifested love—manifested in Jesus Christ.   Only *that* holds our hearts together when He shatters the world."

"Saturday.

"I had finished 'Napoleon,' and was about to write to you on the subject, and I will still write.   Now—'Gregory!'

"'His large hands sway the air about my head.'

"I have read but little lately, and not at all until very lately; but two or three days ago papa held up 'Gregory' before my eyes as something sure to bring pleasure into them.   'Ah! I knew that would move you.'   After all, I have scarcely been long enough face to face with him to apprehend the full grandeur of his countenance.   There are very few grand things, and expounded in your characteristic massiveness of diction. But it does so far appear to me that for the tragic heights, and for that passionate singleness of purpose in which you surpass the poets of our time, we shall revert to ' Cosmo ' and to ' Marlowe.' Well—it may be very wrong —I must think over my thoughts. And at any rate the ' Essay on Tragic Influence ' is full of noble philosophy and poetry. Only you do more honour to the stage and the actorship than I could do. Tragedy is a high form of poetry— perhaps the highest—and absolutely independent, in its own essence, of stages; which involve, to my mind, little more than its translation into a grosser form, in order to its apprehension by the vulgar. What Macready can touch ' Lear ' ? In brief, if the union between tragedy and the gaslights be less incongruous and absurd than the union between Church and State, is it less desecrative of the Divine theory? In the clashing of my *No* against your *Yes*, I must write good-bye.

"Do believe me, under all circumstances, truly and gratefully yours,

E. B. BARRETT.

"Will you tell me when there is any criticism upon 'Gregory' made by οἱ συνετοί, in case I should miss any? I am anxious for the laurels. And you will not be angry that I revert to 'Cosmo'? 'Cosmo' *is* 'Cosmo;' the precedence, were it granted, is only you of you."

III. [Undated, but apparently very soon after the letter from Torquay of May 17th, 1840.]

"It requires some moral courage, dear Mr. Horne, to send you such a present as this cream. But it is of Britannia's Pastorals, and the only fit tribute from

Devonshire—and people like it sometimes in their coffee or tea, or with their fruit. Therefore I pre-forgive your laughing at me.

" ' Gregory ' enlarges while you gaze. Indeed it is a grand production, and one upon which I congratulate both you and our literature.

" The whole of the fourth and fifth acts lies in masses before my admiration, with short interventions. How sublime is the prayer—that one epithet, ' the insufficient sea '—and how much besides, which I can't write of this morning, is not to be forgotten while day follows day. Your Elizabethan fashion of malleting down your metaphors into the ground-work produces a diction of extraordinary power—it is concentrated language.

"Most truly yours,

"ELIZABETH B. BARRETT.

" Torquay, Thursday morning."

IV. [Date faded, but looks like June 30th, 1840.]

" You will think there is no end of me, and *I* am thinking of engaging a secretary to copy out the extracts from Miss Mitford's letters to me, which are addressed to you. Here I send you a page which belongs to you, and is all about your apotheosis in the shape of a geranium at the next Chiswick *fête*. This relates to Mr. Foster's geranium. I had another letter two days ago about a seedling of her own, which is also called after you, and of which both you and I, if we and the sun behave pretty well, are promised a descendant plant next year. And now, dear Mr. Horne, I will let you go in peace.

" Tell me, whenever next you write, both how you are and how the shilling ' Orion ' is going off, for I confess to a curiosity.　　　　　" Yours,

　　　　　　　　" E. B. B.

" Miss Haydon has lost the ' Cartoon prize.' I am so sorry.

" I have explained to Miss Mitford your impossibilities and your probabilities—for the early part of July, I mean."

The new geranium of the Chiswick *fête*, and Miss Mitford's " seedling," which were to be called " Orion," together with the reference to other matters made in the foregoing note, arose in consequence of the friendly interest taken in that gratuitous experiment of the first edition of " Orion " by both these ladies.

The next letter refers to the unusual circumstance of a "hooping-cough" being caught a second time. Having been engaged as one of the Assistant Commissioners in the Government inquiry into the " Employment of Children and Young Persons in Mines and Manufactories," I

chanced one day to be seated for a couple
of hours, during an east wind of the
winter months, taking the evidence of
some children, in a newly plastered
church ante-room, with the accompaniment of a thorough draft from doors and
windows; and a first-rate cough, with all
the " hooping " convulsions, like " laughter holding both his sides " (with a difference), was the consequence. But a much
more important subject, viz., the strug-
gles of an heroic spirit in a most fragile
frame, will be discovered in the following
interesting and touching letter :—

V.   [Post-mark—Torquay, June 12th, 1841.]

" My dear Mr. Horne,—I am so sorry
about the hooping-cough. As a means
of 'rejuvenescence,' why, one might as
pleasantly pass into and through Medea's
kettle. Do try to remember when you
write again, and tell me how you are; if

the change of air perfects the good it has begun. For my own part, I never had the hooping-cough at all. I stood alone in my family, and wouldn't have it when everybody else was hooping.

"I am revived just now—pleased, anxious, excited altogether, in the hope of touching at last upon my last days at this place. I have been up, and bore it excellently—up an hour at a time without fainting—and on several days without injury—and now am looking forward to the journey. My physician has been open with me, and is of opinion that there is a good deal of risk to be run in attempting it. But my mind is made up to go ; and if the power remains to me, I *will* go. To be at home, and relieved from the sense of doing evil where I would soonest bring a blessing—of breaking up poor papa's domestic peace into fragments by keeping my sisters here (and he won't let them leave me)—would urge me into any possible 'risk'—to say nothing of the continual repulsion, night and day, of the sights and sounds of this dreary place. There will be no opposition. So papa promised me at the beginning of last winter that I should go when it became 'possible.' Then Dr. Scully did not talk of 'risk,' but of certain consequences. He said I should die on the road. I know how to understand the change of phrase. There is only a 'risk' now—and the journey is 'possible.' So I go.

"We are to have one of the patent carriages, with a thousand springs, from London, and I am afraid of nothing. I shall set out, I *hope*, in a fortnight.

"Ah, but not directly for London. There is to be some intermediate place where we all must meet, papa says, and stay for a month or two before the final settlement in Wimpole Street,—and he names ' Clifton,' and I pray for the neighbourhood of London, because I look far (too far, perhaps, for me) and fear being left an exile again at those Hot Wells during the winter. I don't know what the ' finality measure' may be. The only thing fixed is a journey from hence :—and ' if I fall,' as the heroes say, why you and ' Psyche' must walk by yourselves. *She*, at least, won't be the worse for it.

"Who taught this parrot its ' How d'ye do?' and so much irrelevancy? You would be tired of me, even if you hadn't the hooping-cough.

"Is it true that Mr. Heraud's magazine is downfallen? And why?

" But don't answer my questions—don't indeed write at all until you are better, and able and inclined to write. Writing is so bad—learning to write is so bad, and I don't suppose that you could write in the way that I do, leaning backwards instead of forwards—lying down, in fact. I write *so* ' to the Horse Guards.'

"How you would smile sarcasms and epigrams out of the ' hood ' if you could see from it what I have been doing, or rather suffering, lately ! Having my picture taken by a lady miniature-painter who wandered here to put an old view of mine to proof. For it wasn't the ruling passion ' strong in death,' ' though by your smiling you may seem to say so,' but a sacrifice to papa.

"Are you tossed about much by the agitation of political matters, or indifferently calm ? I hear nothing from London, except what Lord Melbourne has done, or the Queen said.

" Don't let me mar anything in your conception with regard to the drama. Push any foolishness aside which seems to do it.*

"I did *not* understand your particular view. I thought that our philosopher (Medon), having laboriously worked himself blind with the vain, earthward, cramped strivings of his intellect, was suddenly thrown upon the verge of awaking in, and to, the spiritual world, by a casualty relating to his body itself. It was something of that sort which I seemed to discern in what you wrote.

" Truly yours,

" ELIZABETH B. BARRETT."

Miss Barrett's friendly indignation will

---

* Referring to our mutually projected lyrical drama on the Greek model, an outline of the design of which and the proposed " division of labour " are given in a separate section in the *Post*.

amuse some readers, remembering its cause. I suppose the following is the only " attack upon the Government " to be found in all her writings :—

VI.   " July 24th.

" There was a blank, dear Mr. Horne, in your last notes when you ought to have said something about the cough. I hope the silence meant that you had quite forgotten all the cutting-up and boiling—the whole process of your ' rejuvenescence '— and that your present suffering is concentrated in the parliamentary reports.

" It is an atrocious system altogether— the system established in this England of ours—wherein no river finds its own level, but is forced into leaden pipes, up or down ; her fools lifted into chairs of state, her wise men waiting behind them, and her poets made Cinderellas of, and promoted into accurate counters of pots and pans. We need not wonder at the selections. *Everything* ' is rotten in the state of Denmark.'

" Have you seen Miss Sedgwick's book, and heard the great tempest it has stirred up around you in London, without a Franklin to direct the lightning ? She was received from America two or three years since, by certain societies, with open arms,—none ever suspecting her to be the chiel ' amang them, takin' notes!' The revelation was dreadful. My friend and cousin, Mr. Kenyon—admitted to be one of the most brilliant conversers in London—fell upon the proof-sheets accidentally, just half an hour previous to their publication" (*printing* must be meant), " and finding them sown thick with personalities, side by side with praises of his own agreeable wit, took courage and a pen, and 'cleansed the

premises !'   Afterwards he wrote across
the Atlantic to explain ' the moral right '
he had to his deed.   For my own part,
strongly as I feel the saliency of Miss
Sedgwick's faults (it struck repeatedly
and ungratefully upon some who had bestowed cordial and sisterly attention upon
her, and ' less as an authoress than as a
friend '), I am not quite clear about Mr.
Kenyon's ' right.'   The act was *un peu
fort* in its heroism, and probably his
American admirers may not thank him as
warmly as her victims do.

"Not that I ever do, or could, join
in the outcry against Boswell and his
generation; I like them too well.   But
there is a line—a limit—to their commu-
nicativeness; and such as pass it dirty
their feet.

" Yours,

"E. B. B."

Certainly the feeling of Miss Barrett as
to her cousin's act is the proper one.
Any book or article might be completely
thrown " off its balance " by such a pro-
ceeding. What writer could feel safe if
wholesale and unauthorised erasures could
thus be made in his books? And what
should we think of any printing-office
where it would be permitted?

VII.　　[Postmark—TORQUAY, Aug. 4th, 1841.]

" MY DEAR MR. HORNE,—I am so sorry
to hear of the obstinacy of this cough
of yours. Why do you not get away
from London, and keep moving about?
Continual change of air, says Dr.
Scully—my physician, who says everything of that sort wisely—is the *specific*
for hooping-cough in its advanced stage
— that is, when it lingers as yours
does. Surely you should not allow the

winter months to surprise you coughing. And surely (pardon my impertinence) it wouldn't be much harder to go round London in a circle, if it were only from village to village, previous to the settling down in chambers, than to settle immediately.

"For my own part, I am gasping still for permission to move too; but papa has gone suddenly into Herefordshire, and I am almost sure not to hear for a week. Something, however, must soon be determined; and in the meantime, being tied hand and foot, and gagged, I am wonderfully patient.

"Did you hear of Mrs. Orme's proposal about coming here? It was very kind, and I felt it so, even as an impossibility.

"If you have no 'vow in heaven' *never* to answer a question, will you tell me whether the *Monthly Chronicle* is extinct, and why ?

" Truly yours,

" E. B. B."

VIII.   " TORQUAY, August 14th, 1841.

" I would not hear your enemy say so, dear Mr. Horne, that you were a bad correspondent, much less say so myself. You are a bad *catechumen*, and that's the worst of you, and I'm sure it doesn't deserve a bad cough.   Therefore, if you receive a jar of tamarinds from the West Indies *viâ* Wimpole Street—and you will, in the case of papa's having received any himself, as he usually does—pray use them.   But the pilgrimage through the villages is the remedy.   And never mind 'Psyche.'   There is plenty of time for 'Psyche' in the future, if not now.   She is persecuting you, I fear.   Remember, when one is tied with cords, to struggle only strengthens the knots. Put 'Psyche' away out of thought for the present, and don't fancy that I (for one) am even inclined to be impatient about it. I shall not expect any more news of her for six months, from this fourteenth of August, eighteen hundred and forty-one.

"And so your angelic sin is so rampant that 'you'd be an abbot' (and not a 'butterfly,' despite of 'Psyche') if you went into a monastery—an abbot of misrule—unless St. Cecilia, who 'drew the angel down,' did the like by your reverend desires. Ah! when I was ten years old, I beat you all—you and Napoleon and all—in ambition; but now I only want to get home.

"Nevertheless, I fear I do fear the light words may be bubbles at the top—that it may be darker underneath. I know the secret of that, you see; and I fear that the hooping-cough and the pressure of business don't go blithely together, and that you are walking your imaginary cloisters with a graver, perhaps sadder, step than should be. Can it be so? Is it so? The louder the call then to the villages. Neither cloisters nor graves are ready for you yet, nor you for them. So I do hope that ' generally you don't think' about either. Whom should we have for Dramatic Professor in the great genius establishment [a hit at the Syncretics], where the moth will be sworn never to corrupt, and the thief never to steal? Whom, if you were away? If you were only an abbot, or an organist, it would be very different.

" So, the *Monthly Chronicle* is gone— self-slain, because it wouldn't condescend to be lively. There was power enough in it for three or four magazine popularities

—but the taste of *caviare* preponderated, and people turned away their heads. They said of it, as my own ears witnessed, ' dull and heavy.' Then it was such a fatal mistake to keep back the names! I saw it to the last. God bless you! I am going to think in the face of *the weather*, if it won't turn round.

" Truly yours,

" E. B. B."

The last words convey a more satirical meaning than is apparent.

The brief literary career of the *Monthly Chronicle* is unique, curious, and amusing in a certain way. It was started under the joint auspices of three popular celebrities of the time, Sir David Brewster, Sir E. L. Bulwer, and Dr. Lardner. Being all three proprietors and editors, and each too great to communicate his intentions to either of the others (or even give a defi-

nite reply to the contributor, as I found),
a beautiful confusion was the constant
and necessary result. The magazine,
however, was successfully advancing by
reason of the prestige of the three names,
when the following disastrously natural
event occurred. One wonderful accident
of " Murphy's Almanac " had just burst
through the wintry fogs of London, the
astrologer having truly predicted the very
coldest of all the days of that winter; and
the sale of the Almanac was of a kind
that compelled the publishers (Messrs.
Whittaker) to have police to keep off pur-
chasers from crushing in the door and
windows. The next number of the
Monthly Chronicle, therefore, came out
with a very long article by Sir David
Brewster, " On Murphy's Almanac," and
another article by Dr. Lardner (no ex-
change of ideas having been deigned),

consisting of fourteen pages, "On the Weather," being founded upon the same "Vox Stellarum." They occupied a third part of the whole magazine! After this, the publishers engaged Mr. Robert Bell, who did all that a gallant and indefatigable editor of six feet four could do, but the poor magazine never recovered from that double dose of cold weather.

Miss Barrett's first publication was "An Essay on Mind" (1826); her next was a translation of the "Prometheus" of Æschylos (1833); and her third, "The Seraphim and other Poems," in 1838. A certain critical work in which I was responsibly concerned, while fully admitting her genius, dealt freely with what seemed to be her shortcomings, a *résumé* of which seems to have been condensed in a private note. The following letter will show with how generous a spirit she bore all this :—

IX.   " 50, WIMPOLE STREET,
                   " Nov. 4th, 1841.

" My head has ached so for two days (not my temper, I assure you), that I thought it was beheading itself; and now, that ' distracted globe' having come to a calm, I hasten to answer your letter. A bomb of a letter it is, to be sure! enough to give a dozen poets a headache apiece. ' No sex—no character—no physiognomy —no age—no Anno Domini!'—a very volcano of a letter.

" After all, dear Mr. Horne, your idea of revenge is not tragic enough for a great dramatist, and I may criticise back to you on such grounds. But then, again, I spare you on others. You needn't 'try to recant.' I am not angry—don't even feel ill-used (that feeling of melancholy complacency); and beg you to extend your dramatic sceptre within reach of my subject hands, and with the ' diagram ' at the top of it.*

" When Socrates said that it was worse to suffer, being guilty, than being innocent, wasn't he right,—and am I not like Socrates ?—in the sentiment, which I am right in—not position, which I am wrong in ? At the same time, it does seem hard —hard even for Socrates—to drink all this hemlock without a speech—to die, and make no sign. The general criticism is too true a one, also lately true, but not equally, altogether true, perhaps, in everything. I think, for instance, that my Page-romaunt has some sex and physiognomy, however the Anno Domini

---

* [Referring, probably, to certain geometric figures I had suggested as private " working " illustrations for the " Psyche."]

may be mislaid, even in her case. Well
—but it's a true general criticism—and
true particularly, besides—and do send
the diagram, dear Mr. Horne—and be
sure that however lightly I have spoken,
I must always be gravely grateful to you
for telling me all such truths.

"Miss Mitford came to town last
Thursday, in her abundant affectionate-
ness, just to see me, and returned home
on Saturday. She measures your dramatic stature by cubits. She prefers
your 'Cosmo' to 'Gregory.' So do I,
you know—although the artistic power
is greater in the 'Gregory'—and oh!—
she told me that late struggle of the
unacted authors [the Syncretics] has
done good already in the theatres.
'How?' I asked. 'Because it dis-
proves the late idea of there being an
immense deposit somewhere of excellent

un-acted dramatic works. People say to one another, " You see, they could find nothing more excellent than ' Martinuzzi ;' and thus the theatres open their doors a little wider to the *rare* virtue ! " '

" But you *could* have found something more excellent than ' Martinuzzi.' There was the——; well, but do send the diagram. I wish I could ' transfuse ' in my brother George, who talks of meeting you face to face this evening at Mrs. Orme's.

　　　　　" Truly yours,

　　　　　　" Elizabeth B. Barrett.

" Of course I couldn't object to listen to your arguments upon [against] the title page [of her forthcoming volume], as long as they do not touch my ' foregone conclusions.' But those—pray, dear Mr. Horne, remember—are fixed as Danton's hat."

The next three letters refer principally to the "legitimate drama" and the patent monopoly once possessed by three special London theatres. This is not the place to say much upon the subject. I consider it right that all such monopoly should be destroyed, and (as I put it in the petitions to both Houses) "that every theatre should be permitted to enact the best dramas it could obtain." From the ashes of that monopoly I and those who worked with me at the destruction expected to see a new race both of dramatists and actors arise. Never were sanguine hopes more utterly defeated, and far worse idols were set up in the temples than those which had been cast down. Here was a young lady, living in utter seclusion, and hovering on the brink of the grave, who had far wiser instincts and far keener foresight than the man to whom she was writing with so much deference. She was requested to place her name, among other signatures of eminent persons, to the petition in question.* How must we admire all she said, when we look around at the great majority of the stages of London, knowing what they have spread all over the

---

* My conversation with Bulwer, as to the presentation of our petition to the House of Commons, not having terminated with a definite consent, I had an interview with Mr. Disraeli on the subject, and he handsomely replied, that if Bulwer did not present the petition, he would do so, and request his friend, Lord Lyndhurst, to present the one to the Upper House.

[That Mr. Disraeli, amidst all his multitudinous avocations as a statesman and a novelist, had not forgotten this circumstance after the lapse of even a quarter of a century, is no less remarkable than true. A short time after Mr. Horne's return to England in 1869, he had occasion to write to Mr. Disraeli, who in reply very gracefully reminded Mr. Horne of their old acquaintanceship, alluding especially to their interview respecting the petition against the theatrical patent monopolies.—R. T. M.]

world ever since we destroyed those patent monopolies!—that the "legitimate drama" has been smothered for the last twenty-five years by costly scenes, costly dresses, costly decorations, and licentious dancing; and by burlesques and clap-traps which are an insult to the human understanding, and have proved the ruin of so many deluded managements. The public never craved for such stuff; it was forced upon them, till they came to believe that the British stage was intended to hold the mirror up to Folly and Vulgarity, as the most attractive representations of Art and Nature.

X.   " Torquay [not dated, but the postmark looks like 1841].

"Nothing of the 'tragic subject' to-day, dear Mr. Horne: I am going to get into a scrape instead.

"I tremble to do it, take a long breath

before I begin, and then beg you to excuse me about the signature, and forgive me, if possible, afterwards.

"Have I done it? Is it all over with me? Oh! I feel the shadow of the great Gregory's hand, to match the foot, even at this distance.*

"As to the petition, the justice of the claim lies upon the surface, and its policy not much deeper, and therefore in writing, and predicting all success, I need not stir from the common sense of the question. You are sure to gain the immediate object, and you ought to do so, even though the ultimate object remain as far off as ever, and more evidently far. There is a deeper evil than licenses or the want of licenses—the base and blind public taste. Multiply your theatres, and license

---

* Alluding to what is said, in my tragedy, of the hand and foot of Hildebrand.

every one—do it to-day—and the day
after to-morrow (you may have one night)
there will come Mr. Bunn, and turn out
you and Shakespeare with a great roar of
lions. Well! we shall see.

"You know far more than I do, and
you seem to hope more. If the great
mass in London were Athenians, I might
hope too. But I do *not* like giving my
name to anything about the theatres. It
is a name unimportant to everybody in
the world except just myself, for whom
the giving of it would be the sign of an
opinion; and I should not like to give
it in any one thing favourable to the
theatres. At their best, take the ideal of
them, and the soul of the Drama is far
above the stage; and according to present
and perhaps all past regulations in this
country, dramatic poetry has been dese-
crated into the dust of our treading,—yes,

and too often forced to desecration, and
drawn down morally in turn, by the stage.
When the poet has his gods in the gallery, what must be the end of it?　Why,
that even Shakespeare should bow his
starry head oftener than Homer nodded,
and write down his pure genius into the
dirt of the groundlings, for the sake of the
savour of their 'most sweet voices;' and
even so be outwritten in popularity for
years and years by his half-brother noble
geniuses, Beaumont and Fletcher, *because*
they stooped still lower.

" Well, but if you strike your head
ever so much over this, and call me ever
so many names, don't be really angry.
People will have their fancies and per-
versities,—grant me mine.　If the name
you asked for were not ' bosh,' I should
be still more sorry than I now am to say
no to your asking.　And yet, even as it

is, I didn't like writing—either yesterday or the day before—nor do I to-day.

"The *Monthly Chronicle* has not reached me yet. I am eager for the added scene of ' Cosmo.'

"And glad, dear Mr. Horne, that you could like anything in the volume where there is more to forgive than like, for even the kindest.

"Ever truly yours,

"E. B. B."

XI.   " Torquay [no date given].

" Thank you, dear Mr. Horne, for the *Statesman*, which is returned by the present post. So, dramatists can't originate under the Guelphs—can't 'call their souls their own '—and nothing *is* originated in your tragedies. Such nonsense shouldn't provoke us as it does—*but* it does.

"Now, there is that Mr. Darley who

has written a ' Dramatic Chronicle '
(' Thomas à Becket '), to prove that,
nature being exhausted, there can be no
more tragedies. No; the ' Chronicle '
was not written to prove it: the Preface
was. But he might more safely have
left it to the ' Chronicle '—Q. E. D. A
clever, picturesque composition—powerful in a certain way, though not in the
tragic. If Mr. Darley stood alone as a
tragedian, his proposition would be irre-
futable. Not that I disesteem him. He
wrote a beautiful tuneful pastoral once
—' Sylvia, or the May Queen '—but the
missing thing is passion—pathos—if not
a *besides*.

" How wonderful that such ideas should
be taken up by people with one ! *

---

* Part of this denunciation is attributable to a
friendly championship ; Mr. Darley, it was said, having
attacked me in a critical journal. Justice is done to
his pastoral poem, but only a stinted justice to some

" But as to *poetry*, they are all sitting (in mistake), just now, upon Caucasus for Parnassus—and wondering why they don't see the Muses! He hasn't a heart even for Beaumont and Fletcher; and, to his mind, the cause of the abundance of poetical genius in the old times was—the difficulty they had in writing. We spell too well for anything! Here's a discovery!

" It comes to this. If poetry, under any form, be exhaustible, Nature is; and

of his dramatic writing. In one of his Chronicles there is a fight described between the High Chancellor, "tower-heavy Turketul," and " Gorm," a Scandinavian sea-king, worthy of the most heroic bardic power. Turketul at last strikes Gorm a finishing blow with his mace, and merely makes this terribly grim comment upon the affair—

" Fell—laughed—and died! he made a goodly end!"

The letter alludes in a complimentary way to the critical journal in which Mr. Darley was writing his dramatic heresies, though I got him to sign our petition, notwithstanding.

if Nature be—we are near a blasphemy—
I, for one, could not believe in the im-
mortality of the soul.

> ' Si l'ame est immortelle,
> L'amour ne l'est-il pas ? '

Extending *l'amour* into all love of the
ideal, and attendant power of idealizing.

"But, ah! there may be another mistake! Do you fancy that directly you
have opened the minor theatres, 'Cosmos'
and 'Gregories,' unwritten by you, will
pour through the doors? *I* don't. I
don't believe in mute inglorious Miltons,
and far less in mute inglorious Shake-
speares. Van Amburgh's new elephant
will take turn with 'Gregory the Seventh'
—you will see.

"Where do you go in July? for *me*, I
can't answer. I am longing to go to
London, and hoping to the last. For the
present—certainly the window has been

opened twice—an inch—but I can't be lifted even to the sofa without fainting. And my physician shakes his head or changes the conversation, which is worse, whenever London is mentioned. But I do grow stronger ; and if it becomes possible, I shall go, WILL go! That sounds better, doesn't it. Putting it off to another summer is like a ' never.'

"I was so glad to have your note. I really thought you had gone to America, or were tired of me—worse still. I never thought of ' neglect,' that being such a wrong word—but, otherwise, I lie here fancying all sorts of things in heaven and earth.

"It is a shame to expect all this stuff to be read by any person with time filled up as yours must be. Never mind throwing aside what I write for your leisure. Never let me be in the way.

Now, if you are tired, you are avenged,
for I am too.

"Ever truly,

"E. B. B."

XII.   "Torquay [no date, but probably 1842].

"My dear Mr. Horne,—Thank you for
the reproof from Hazlitt—in paragraph
'to suit'—for beauty is the gentleness of
the rebuke. Yet you and he could both
have written as finely and forcibly upon
the oposite evil of compromise [as to the
theatrical patents], of temporising as to
objects, and being indifferent to means—
that 'fat weed' of the day—perhaps of
the world on all days. More of us, you
will admit, do harm by groping along the
pavement with blind hands for the beggar's brass coin, than do folly by clutching
at the stars 'from the misty mountain-
top.' And if the would-be star-catchers

catch nothing, they keep at least clean fingers.

"This applies to nothing, you will understand, except to the passage from Hazlitt—suggestively.

"And talking of beggar's coins, will you believe me (you MUST believe me) that I never thought until I had finished my letter to you about the petition, of my own self having something to do with the proprietorship of Drury Lane, by virtue of five shares given to me when I was a child? I really never thought of it. But I thought afterwards that if you ever came to guess at such a thing, why you might infer me into basenesses. The shares never reminded me of their being mine by one penny coming to my hands, nor are likely to do so—the national theatres being as empty of profit as of honour. But if it were otherwise, you couldn't suspect me of being warped by such a consideration—you will trust me that half-cubit of probity, without another word.

" E. B. B."

XIII.   [With pen-and-ink profile of Keats at head.]
" Dec. 29th, 1842.

" Tell me, Mr. Horne—is it like? to Keats, I mean. My hands have the ague this morning. Otherwise it would be a copy of a sketch of Keats; and I want to know if you have any recognition. For my own part, my observation is— I am afraid almost of saying it—that there is a resemblance between the mouth in this sketch and that which I blasphemed against in a certain miniature —resolute fifth-act lips! Do confess— supposing that you preserve for me any common degree of patience—whether any one in the world ever detected a likeness between the two poets in question.

"The world is better than I imagined, and since I wrote to you about book-sellers, I have had an inkling of a reason for believing what I had not faith for pre-viously, that in the case of my resolving to deliver up a volume of poems to my own former publisher, he would print it 'without being paid for it.' And now perhaps I *shan't* print it, out of the spirit of contradiction.

"Ever and truly,

"E. B. B."

XIV.   "June 14th, 1843.

"My DEAR MR. HORNE,—I have read and forwarded your letter to Miss Mitford —who tells me in a letter yesterday (a cross-stitch), that in spite of all I can say, she is glad of having written to you, because you '*will be obliged to say some-*

thing in your answer.' Well! I also am glad that somebody is curious besides myself; and I am not sorry that the somebody should be herself, being jealous of her 'with Styx nine times round me,' in natural proportion to her degree of glory and victory and twenty-five promised copies!

"Very well, Mr. Horne!

"'It is quite useless,' said I to Miss Mitford, 'that you should make *your* application! *Have I not asked for six copies, and been refused?'* Now carry the result of the application historically downwards—and me with it!

"As to your suggestion about the compromise of her and my struggling heroically for these *spolia opima*—really, you can know little of what heroes, female heroes, are made, to suggest such a thing! I have told Miss Mitford (to disabuse you

at once) that not if she and you asked me
on your four knees to touch a page of the
twenty-five would I consent to such a
thing—I make feminine oath against it—
I DON'T CHOOSE TO DO IT. I won't have one
of them—no, nor of any others in their
stead.

" Very well, Mr. Horne !

" After all, it is not (seriously) so very
ill; because she may have (has probably)
twenty-five or more ' learned and accomplished friends,' and I have not; and Mr.
Miller will probably be in a better humour
in a second edition than his advertisement
gives us present hope of; and I recognise
at once the fact that you should not be
asked to give your books away actually as
a consequence of your doing so virtually.
Virtually—not virtuously. Not in the
least do I approve of your distributing the
second edition in the manner of the first.

The cause of it, and the object in it, are inscrutable to me—particularly as I don't hold to the common opinion that much poetry has made the author mad. Papa says, 'Perhaps he is going to shoot the Queen, and is preparing evidence of monomania'—an ingenious conjecture, but not altogether satisfactory.

"I have seen no criticism at all. The star-gazers will all have their glasses up, of course, 'while this new planet swims into their ken.' But 'Orion' is a con-stellation, isn't he?

"Pity my astronomy, if not my ill-temper—which last may not be quite so bad as it seems.

"Ever yours,
"E. B. B."

The next letter was written under the influence of a sadness, the cause of which is not expressed; it also refers to some matters connected with the gratuitous circulation of " Orion." *

XV.   "WIMPOLE STREET,
            "June 16th, 1843.

" I am sorry, my dear Mr. Horne, at your remaining unwell against all my hopes, but I am more sorry than I was this morning at having written a very silly note to you a few days since.

" That it was simply silly—meaning that it wasn't *seriously* silly, I beg you to believe. I am apt to write the thought or the jest—as it may be—which is uppermost—and sometimes, too, when it is

---

* Published originally at a nominal price, to save the author the expense and trouble of sending copies to his numerous friends. Mr. Horne made two stipulations with his publisher: first, that no person should be supplied with more than one copy; and secondly, that no copy should be sold to any person who called it " Orïon."—S. R. T. M.

not uppermost; I struggle against a sadness which is strong, by putting a levity in the place of it. Now you will wonder what I have been writing, if you have not received the note yet—and so I will explain to you that it was only some foolishness about the twenty-five copies—about Miss Mitford's victory, and my defeat, $\kappa. \tau. \lambda.$

" My grave and real thoughts are these, that I think you exceedingly kind to both of us—kinder than you ought to be. And then she has more in her power—she can do more for the poem — she counts an amount of learned and accomplished friends above any person I ever knew or heard of. And for a good private advertiser, never was any one superior to her own self. For which reasons I would rather give up the whole twenty-five copies to her, and so I have told her,

without a reserve of five or one for myself.
I have one copy from you already, which
I keep in my covetousness, as your gift,
and the few others I require shall be
arrived at by your instructions from this
second edition—or the twenty-second.
On the success of the poem I congratulate
you and everybody worthy of the joy of it.
Still the very success must be loss in a
certain way—and I cannot help wishing
that it had been otherwise.

"Ever truly yours,

"E. B. B."

XVI.   July 7th, 1843.

"The lady's name is Cockell, Miss
Cockell, Katherine Cockell, and she lives
in Livonia Cottage, about a mile from
Sidmouth, in Devonshire, where we re-
sided once for two years. She was an
invalid, poor thing, then, and sent to ask
me to go to see her—which I did at great

expense of shyness. But *that* you won't believe, because, as Mr. Kenyon says, I grow insolent when I have a pen in my hand, and you know me only 'by that sign.' I sometimes doubt to myself (do you know, besides) whether if I should ever be face to face with you, the shame and the shyness would not annihilate the pleasure of it to me! I really think they would—but this is not what I was going to say.

"Poor Miss C—— was always an interesting person in my eyes. She is full of enthusiasm of heart, which overflows itself over all things—and then I believe her to be very, very solitary in the most painful sense—desolate in her affections —left alone without an answering sympathy. I do not know the particular circumstances; and once, when she was inclined to enter on them, I begged her,

observing the pain it gave her, not to go
on; this anatomising of life-diseases by
retrospection being dreadful and useless.
But I see that she is very unhappy—or
rather, that she has been much afflicted—
and that the shadow of the sorrow and
an actual most desolate solitude are with
her now. She has a fine apprehension of
beauty and greatness, as you perceive, a
sensitiveness of the spiritual sense, and a
natural exaltation, perfectly unaffected
and un-put-on. Once she said to me
what I never shall forget. Making an
ungenerous inference from the fact of
pain being connected with the affections,
I had observed that I would refuse to
know anybody, man, woman, or child,
whom I was likely to love and be loved
by intensely. 'Oh,' she said, 'is it possible you can say so? I would walk like
a pilgrim to the end of the world to find

one who would love me and whom I could love.' That was the true feeling—generous and worthy of love, and I recognised it when I heard it, just as we recognise the right word in a flowing poem, which the memory had missed, when it is spoken suddenly before us. And she is full of such instincts. I mean to send your note to her, because it is sure to give her pleasure; and as you had hers, it is only fair that she should have yours in turn.

"By the way, you have charmed Miss Mitford by your last note of acceptance of her hospitalities.

" 'A charming note,' she calls it. And so you are going to enact 'Orion' with the harp under the bay-tree! I am very glad of it. And by the way, again, you are gracious to our sex in receiving her remark upon what women do in opposition to what men do—and perhaps just. Certainly the discrimination of the beautiful is the art of criticism,—and not the finding of faults. And therefore her remark and your consent to it would prove women to be generally better judges of poetry, because more sensitive to the faculty than men are. Of this I cannot help doubting a little. How many bright eyes, yes, and 'beautiful smiles' besides, I have known, to whom poetry is really nothing, startles me when I think of it— it is such a playing at cross-purposes with nature! That 'beautiful smile' we both know, which will grow more radiant for music, fades away out of its own gloriole at any talk about poetry. Be sure that the poetical sense, even in *apprehension,* is a rare thing among men, and among women not less so.

"Mr. Kenyon was with me yesterday, and praised 'Orion' most admiringly.

He had read it only in parts yet, through a press of occupation, but he had from these parts, he said, the same sort of pleasure as from Keats's ' Endymion ' or ' Hyperion;' and what particularly charmed him was the versification. He accused me of the *Athenæum* paper, and convicted me against my will; and when I could no longer deny, and began to explain and ' pique myself upon my diplomacy,' he threw himself back into his chair, and laughed me to scorn as the least diplomatic of his acquaintance. ' *You* diplomatic ! '

" Truly yours,

" E. B. B.

" Mr. Kenyon said, besides the rest, ' Orion has very much raised my opinion of Mr. Horne's power.' "

XVII. "July 13, 1843.

" DEAR MR. HORNE,—I return the magazines and letters, with thanks to you for the great pleasure which in many ways they have given to me. I am a sort of believer in handwriting divination, and took interest in the very shapes of their respective alphabets,—and then it is delightful to see how the feeling for ' Orion ' spreads and deepens in all classes and minds — how not a single note of the octave, along which you trailed your finger, is dumb or responseless. Yes, that last review does you fuller justice than the others—indeed, very full justice, as it seems to me. But won't the *Westminster Review* speak out, as it ought ? Won't your friends of the *Church of England Quarterly* help you in anywise ? And will no one climb to the heights of the *Edinburgh* with the new epic in his hand? These are wishes rather than questions. I will be innocent of teasing you to-day.

" Sincerely yours,

"ELIZABETH B. BARRETT.

" Shyness imply *doubt?* Surely not—except it be doubt of oneself. But it is a species of consciousness which is, as Miss Mitford observes wisely, resolvable into self-love, subtilise about it as we may. Only perhaps in some cases, and where there is no reserve of character to *background* it, the nerves, considered physically, should be justly obliged to bear the blame. I hope so, but do not know it. One thing I know, that I cannot be innocent of teasing you, let my resolutions set in ever so well!

" Adieu — you won't hear from me again these two months to come."

It has been mentioned that, at the request of Miss Barrett, I contributed to an Annual edited by Miss Mitford, and as this was the means of my introduction to the authoress of " Our Village," who is referred to in the next letter, it may be as well at this point to give the reader my recollections of that charming and accomplished lady.

There used to be, and there no doubt still is, if I had but the courage to go and look at it, a small, old-fashioned cottage at Three-mile Cross, near Reading, which stood in a garden close to the road. A strip of garden was on one side, a little pony-stable on the other, and the larger part of the garden at the back. It was a comfortable-looking, but still a real village cottage, with no town or suburb look whatever about it. Small lattice windows, below and above, with roses and

jasmine creeping round them all, established its rural character; and there was
a great buttress of a chimney rising from
the ground at the garden-strip side, which
was completely covered with a very
ancient and very fine apricot tree. There
the birds delighted to sit and sing among
the leaves, and build too, in several snug
nooks, and there in early autumn the
wasps used to bite and bore into the rich
ripe brown cracks of the largest apricots,
and would issue forth in rage when any
one of the sweetest of their property was
brought down to the earth by the aid of a
clothes-prop, guided under the superin-
tending instructions of a venerable little
gentlewoman in a garden-bonnet and
shawl, with silver hair, very bright hazel
eyes, and a rose-red smiling countenance.
Altogether, it was one of the brightest
faces any one ever saw.

" Now, my dear friend," would she say,
" if you will only attend to my advice,
you will get that apricot up there, which
is quite in perfection. I have had my
eye upon it these last three weeks,
wondering nobody stole it. The boys
often get over into the garden before any
of us are up. There now, collect all
those leaves, if you will be so good—and
those too—and lay them all in a heap
just underneath, so that the apricot may
fall upon them. If you don't do that, it
will burst open with a thump. There!
now push the prop up slowly, so as to
break the apricot from the stalk; and
when it is down, do not be in too great a
hurry to take it up, as it's sure to have a
good large wasp or two inside. Wasps
are capital judges of ripe wall-fruit, as
my dear father used to say. A little
lower with the prop!—more to the left—.

now just push the prong upwards, and
gently lift—again—down it comes ! Mind
the wasps !—three, four—mind !—perhaps
that's not all—five !—I told you so ! "

" How angry they are ! "

" Not more, my dear friend, than you
and I would have been under similar circumstances."

I had not known Miss Mitford very long
at this time; but it was her habit to
address all those with whom she was
on intimate terms, by some affectionate
expression. For several years, however,
I used to pay a visit of a week or ten days
to Miss Mitford's cottage during the
strawberry season, and again during the
middle of summer, when her show of
geraniums (she resisted all new nomen-
clatures) was at its height, and sometimes
later, when the wonderful old fruit-trees
just retained some half-dozen of their

choicest treasures. It would be impossible for any engraving or photograph, however excellent as to features, to convey a true likeness of Mary Russell Mitford. During one of these visits, Miss Charlotte Cushman was also staying at the cottage, and exclaimed the first time Miss Mitford left the room, "What a bright face it is!" This effect of summer brightness all over the countenance was quite remarkable. A floral flush overspread the whole face, which seemed to carry its own light with it, for it was the same indoors as out. The silver hair shone, the forehead shone, the cheeks shone, and, above all, the eyes shone. The expression was entirely genial, cognoscitive, beneficent. The outline of the face was an oblate round, of no very marked significance beyond that of an apple, or other rural "character;" in fact, it was very like a rosy apple in the sun. Always excepting the forehead and chin. The forehead was not only massive, but built in a way that sculpture only could adequately delineate. Miss Barrett, in a note to a friend concerning Miss Mitford, described her forehead as of the ancient Greek type, and compared it to her idea of *Akinetos*, or the Great Unmoved,* although we may doubt whether the amiable authoress of "Our Village" would have felt very much pleased or complimented by the unexpected comparison. Howbeit, this brainstructure accounted to me for the fact that Miss Mitford's conversation was often very superior to anything in her books. Having on one occasion suggested this, she said, smiling: "Well, you see, my dear friend, we must take the world

* In Mr. Horne's poem of "Orion."—ED.

as we find it, and it doesn't do to say to everybody, all that you would say to one here and there." And presently afterwards, when alluding to several persons, without mentioning any names, for she was a very politic lady of the old school, Miss Mitford added : " One has to think twice before speaking once, in order to come down to them ; like talking to children."

This build of head, and strong outline of head and face, will go far to explain the strength of character displayed by Miss Mitford during the early and most trying periods of her life, with her extravagant and selfish father. It may also equally account for her general composure and presence of mind, both on great occasions and others, trifling enough to talk and write about, but of a kind to test the nerves of most ladies. For instance, in driving Miss Mitford one day in her little pony-chaise on a morning visit, she so riveted my attention on the special point of a story, that I allowed one wheel to run into a dry ditch at the roadside, and the pony-chaise must of course have turned over, but that we were "brought up" by the hedge. "Hillo! my dear friend!" said Miss Mitford; "we must get out." We did so; the little trap was at once put on its proper course, and, without one word of comment, the bright-faced old lady took up the thread of her story.

Her favourite seat in the cottage, in the garden, and in the large greenhouse where she received visitors during the "strawberry season" (her usual definition of certain months) I have not revisited, and had better never do so.

In the next letter there are more half-veiled allusions to "Psyche," and to a certain report in one of the Government blue-books.*

XVIII. "August 7th, 1843. Monday.

"I *did* guess a little that when you were talking mysteriously, you were talking *psycho*logically. And also, from the silence afterwards, I inferred before you stated the fact to me, that the intention failed again by the fatality. Be sure that the Fates are sworn against us—be as sure of it as I am! For the immediate failure I am not sorry; having one or two poems of different sizes (none very large) on my hands; and being rather bent on preparations for that volume of my own, which, in its undeveloped state, has already served to illustrate its author's self-will.

* Mr. Horne's Report on the "Employment of Children in Mines and Manufactories "—S. R. T. M.

If you ever look into *Blackwood*, condescend this month to look at *me*. Because my 'Cry of the Children' owes its utterance to your exciting causations. To-day I shall see your 'Old Problem,'* of which the critics do prophesy good things. I salute 'Orion' in the fifth edition.

"At four o'clock to-morrow you will be at Three-mile Cross, and at four o'clock to-day I shall be peradventure in my chair for the second time. When I write to tell Miss Mitford vaingloriously that the ivy planted in a box in my window-sill has taken root, flourished, and spread itself in green boughs and tendrils over the window, until I sit in the green light of the woods, she answers (oh, hard of

* A poem by Mr. Horne, which appeared in Douglas Jerrold's *Illuminated Magazine*, with a large vignette by Kenny Meadows, of the "Poet, the Stoic, and the Fool," in one united or tri-unal head.—S. R. T. M.

heart!) that she has roses round *her* window. There is the like analogy in our fates, yours and mine,—and we think to write ' Psyches ' together!

" I heard of 'Orion' the other day being admired at the first glance, and carried away to be admired at leisure, by Mrs. Jameson. You admire Mrs. Jameson, I am sure, as I do, and will be sensitive to her admiration. She has a fine aspiring spirit—noble instinct for greatness—and she can write very eloquently. Is 'Orion in the fiftieth edition !!

" Do tell me how you are pleased, and exactly how you are impressed by the visit to Three-mile Cross. I will be secret beyond womanity, if you are frank beyond discretion. Barter your impressions with me, my dear Mr. Horne.

" Ever truly yours,

" ELIZABETH B. BARRETT."

The next letter is valuable for the opinion it expresses of Harriet Martineau, from whom not long since I received a note written whilst lying in a similar state to that described by Miss Barrett with such simple and pathetic grandeur in 1843.

XIX.   " August 31st, 1843.

[Apparently from Wimpole Street.]

"Ah, my dear Mr. Horne, while you are praising the weather—stroking the sleek sunshine—it has been, not exactly killing me, but striking me vigorously with intent to kill. It was intensely hot, and I went out in the chair, and was over-excited and over-tired, I suppose; at least, the next day I was ill, shivering in the sun, and lapsing into a weariness it is not easy for me to rally from. Yet everybody has been ill—which, in the way of pure benevolence, ought to be a comfort

to me; and now I am well again. And
the weather is certainly lovely and bright
by fits, and I join you in praising the
beauty and glory of it : but then, you
must admit that the *fits*, the spasmodic
changes of the temperature from sixty-
one degrees to eighty-one, and back
again, are trying to mortal frames, more
especially to those conscious of the frailty
of the 'native mud' in them. If I had
the wings of a dove, and could flee away
to the south of France, I should be
cooing peradventure instead of moaning.
Only, I could not *leave everything*—
even then! I must stay, as well as go
—under any circumstances — dove or
woman.

"By the way, two of my brothers are
on the Rhine at this moment. They
have gone, to my pain and pleasure, to
see Geneva, and come home at the end

of six weeks, by Paris, to re-plunge (one of them) into law.

"It pleases me to think of dear Miss Mitford reading my ' House of Clouds ' to you, with her ' melodious feeling ' for poetry, and the sweeter melody of her kindliness; and it moreover pleased me to know that you liked it in any measure. To show the difference of possible opinions, Mr. Boyd told me that ' he had read my papers on the Greek fathers ' [in the *Athenæum*, I think], 'with the more satisfaction, because he had inferred from my "House of Clouds" that illness had *impaired my faculties.*' Ah, but I hope to do something yet, better than the past. I hope, and shall struggle to it.

"I have had a great pleasure lately in some correspondence with Miss Martineau, the noblest female intelligence between the seas,—' as sweet as spring, as ocean deep.' She is in a hopeless anguish of body, and serene triumph of spirit, with at once no hope and all hope! To hear from her was both a pleasure and honour to me.

"Last week a voice spake to me out of a beautiful smile—'Ask Mr. Horne if he has given me up for ever, and tell him that I still live at E—— S——.'

"Very truly yours,

"ELIZABETH B. BARRETT."

We will conclude this first of the series of Letters by a choice morsel of graphic criticism on a certain clerical celebrity,—showing how that frail little arm, being put forth from a sofa, could wield a gleaming broadsword, and strike home, either with impassioned eye, or, as in the present instance, with a forehead beaming with mixed indignation and irony.

XX.   "WIMPOLE STREET,
                                 "Dec. 16th, 1843.

"I am so glad to hear that nothing really very bad is the matter with Tennyson. If anything were to happen to Tennyson, the world should go into mourning.

. "Did I ever tell you that I once wrote to him, and had a note from him? Thus it was. Some friendly American sent me last year a newspaper, containing a review of his poetry, and requested me to forward it to him, knowing my direction, and not his. I was embarrassed to know what to do; and more especially so as the review was cautious in its admiration. At last I wrote a brief statement of the facts of the case, and sent the newspaper. I was quite ashamed of myself and my newspaper; but he was good enough to forgive me for an involuntary

forwardness. The people in Yankeeland,
I observe, think that we in England all
live in a house together—particularly we
who write books. The idea of the absence of forests and savannahs annihi-
lates with them the idea of distance.

" I am content—in relation to poetry—
I can understand perfectly. Perhaps,
however, you have underrated certain
perceptions of an individual, of poetry
in its highest order. The individual in
my mind (probably different from the
individual in yours) can appreciate Tennyson, Wordsworth, Keats, and your
'Cosmo.' Still, I admit that I should
shrink a little from the suggested hot
ploughshare of your magnificent

' Oblivion, crown'd with infinite blank stars ; '

because certainly there is a mystical
effluence of poetry (a highest height
over the highest height) in Words-

worth, Tennyson, Keats, which escapes the individuality of *my* individual—always did, and must. But now, I think, we have written into about as thick a fog as obliged us to light the candles at noon a few days since. Only I don't mean to light the candles here.

"I have not the *Blackwood* in question. I could send for the number, but cannot remember definitely. I think it came out just after the ' Seraphim '—in 1839, was it not ?—and I think the paper called itself ' Our Two Vases,' that being a current title of a series of critical papers by Christopher North. Mr. Milnes and I were reviewed together in the paper I refer to, and we had it to ourselves.

"No—I did not suppose that the opinion I sent to you amounted to much ; but I will send you one, since you care to have it. Also, he and I were associated together with Mr. Sterling, and one or two more *Blackwood* poets, in the *North American Review* of last year. Mr. Milnes was treated unworthily in it, I think, and overthrown for want of imagination and fire. They behaved very generously to me, and, after sundry admonitions, unquestionably founded, dismissed me with a laurel-branch. This paper was written, I have since ascertained, by the Head of Harvard College, Boston—or perhaps 'ascertained' may be too hard and self-satisfied a word—say 'believed' instead.

" So, Tennyson is 'pretty,' is he? Did I ever tell you that I heard a lady—a countess—by the order of St. Louis!—say, 'The latter part of Homer is certainly very pretty'? These are your critics, O Israel!

" For my own part, I was going to

observe (when I last wrote to you) that I should be satisfied, in the case of a certain moral enmity, with such an execration as, ' Oh, that mine enemy would write a book ! ' I stopped the pen, because it struck me as too savage. I will say it now, though.

" Mr. Lough is engaged on a bust of poor Southey, which is said to be fine, and resembling. His widow went to see it the other day.

" The anonymous 'Life in the Sick Room,' by an invalid, is by Miss Martineau, and worthy of her; full of noble Christian philosophy, and most affecting, through its very calmness.

" I cannot write any more—which is lucky, I believe.

" Yours truly,
"E. B. B."

" You will be glad to hear that dear Miss Mitford has been chosen Honorary Member of the new Literary Institute, under Buckingham. They have also chosen Agnes Strickland, to prevent any unpleasantness to Miss Mitford, from the circumstance of her being the only woman.

" Talking of poets—no, not talking of poets, but thinking of poets—are you aware, O Orion, that the most popular poet alive is the Reverend Robert Montgomery, who walks into his twenty and somethingth edition 'like nothing'? I mean the author of ' Satan;' ' Woman;' ' Omnipresence of the Diety;' ' The Messiah;' the least of these being in its teens of editions, and the greatest not worth a bark of my Flushie's! Mr. Flushie is more of a poet, by the shining of his eyes! But is it not wonderful that this man who waves his white handkerchief from the pulpit till the tears run in rivulets all round, should have another trick of oratory (as good) where he can't show the ring on his little finger? I really do believe that the 'Omnipresence of the Deity' is in the twenty-fourth edition, or beyond it,—a fact that cannot be stated in respect to Wordsworth after all these years."

II.

"Chaucer Modernized."

II.

" CHAUCER MODERNIZED."

Origin of the Work—I accept the Editorship—My Col-
laborators—Miss Barrett's Qualifications for the task
she undertook—Wordsworth's and Landor's Opinion
—Bulwer's View—The Principle adopted—Leigh
Hunt's Dissent from it—Specimens of Miss Barrett's
Version of "The Complaint of Annelida"—Her
Method of arranging the Rhymes—Miss Barrett's
Opinion of her Coadjutors' work—Specimens of
Printers' Proofs with marginalia—Leigh Hunt's
Broad Theory—Translations of Shelley, Oxenford
and Denis Florence MacCarthy—Recollections of
Robert Bell—Thackeray.

IN 1841, a project was set on foot (by
Wordsworth, I believe) for giving the
world, for the first time, a true yet polished
modernization of the Father of English
Poetry. All previous so-called modernizations of Chaucer (with the single exception of Lord Thurlow's rendering of

the " Knight's Tale ") had been, at best, paraphrases, *ad libitum* translations, or gross parodies and desecrations of the homely power, beauty, graphic richness, and quaint humour of the original. Of the fact that Chaucer was not only a versifier of wonderful variety, but that (so far as we can discover and imagine the actual quantities he used and intended us to read) he was a master of versification, and this in himself, and without considering the age in which he wrote, not the remotest recognition had ever been shown. It was agreed that this project should be carried out by Wordsworth, Leigh Hunt, Miss Barrett, Robert Bell, Monckton Milnes, Dr. Leonhard Schmitz, and myself. Some difficulty was experienced in the choice of an editor. Wordsworth, being in years, and residing at a distance, would not accept the post.

The next in seniority was Leigh Hunt,
who was living near London, and in all
respects suitable as a most accomplished
reader and lover of Chaucer. But he was
too wise; he "smelt the battle afar off;"
and, as Wordsworth, to whom several
of us had sent poems we had modernized,
had written to London to say that my
rendering of "The Franklin's Tale" was
"as well done as any lover of Chaucer's
poetry need or can desire," * the editor-

* [In a letter to Mr. Henry Reed of Philadelphia
("Memoirs of William Wordsworth." By Christopher
Wordsworth, D.D., 1851, Vol. ii., pp. 375), Wordsworth says—"There has recently been published in
London a volume of some of Chaucer's tales and poems
modernized. This little specimen originated in what
I attempted with the 'Prioress's Tale;' and if the
book should find its way to America you will see in
it two further specimens from myself. Let me re-
commend to your notice the 'Prologue' and the
'Franklin's Tale;' they are both by Mr. Horne, a
gentleman unknown to me, but are, the latter in particular, very well done."—S. R. T. M.]

ship was offered to me. To my subsequent regret, hard work, waste of time
in verbal conflicts, countless vexations—
yet pride, withal—I accepted the office,
" little dreaming."

After the first volume had been satis-
factorily launched, a second was contem-
plated, for which it was intended to request the co-operation of Tennyson, Talfourd, Browning, Sir E. L. Bulwer, Mr.
and Mrs. Cowden Clarke, and Mary
Howitt.

Miss Barrett, though still supposed to
be hovering near the grave, cheerfully,
and with enthusiasm, agreed to lend her
aid to the work. And it is a great pleasure to recollect that everybody to whom
I applied cordially consented, with the
exception of Landor, who, however, ob-
jected in a form that could not be dis-
pleasing to those engaged in this labour

of love. His first reply was that he believed " as many people read Chaucer" (meaning in the original) " as were fit to read him." As I took leave to doubt this, Landor again wrote saying—"Indeed I *do* admire him, or rather love him. In my opinion, he is fairly worth a score or two of Spensers. He had a knowledge of human nature, and not of doll-making and *fantoccini* dressing. 'Imagination' seems to our poets and critics to be the faculty of devising a rare quantity of small images." Adding—"Pardon me if I say I would rather see Chaucer quite alone, in the dew of his sunny morning, than with twenty clever gentlefolks about him, arranging his shoe-strings and buttoning his doublet. I like even his *language.* I will have no hand in breaking his dun but rich-painted glass, to put in (if clearer) much thinner panes."

And thus,—with the true, but narrow, devotion of the best men on the black-letter side, and their resistance to all attempts to melt the obsolete language and form it into modern moulds,—and the stolidity of a British public on another side, the Homer of English Poetry continues unread, except by very few. Had Chaucer's poems been written in Greek or Hebrew, they would have been a thousand times better known—they would have been translated again and again, year after year.*

Writing to Sir E. L. Bulwer, the principle I proposed for acceptance was, that the best way of doing the work would be gracefully and poetically to retain as much of the original language of Chaucer as possible. Wordsworth had at once coincided in this; so had Miss Barrett,

* [See the Introduction by R. H. Horne.—ED.]

and so did all the rest but Leigh Hunt, who did not altogether coincide. And the more he worked at the modernization, the less he agreed with that principle, and I fully admit there is much to be said for his view of the matter.

We all commenced. Wordsworth gave a version of "The Cuckoo and the Nightingale," an extract from "Troilus and Cressida," and virtually modernized the whole of "The Flower and the Leaf," by the re-writings and general labour he bestowed upon it for somebody else. Leigh Hunt modernized "The Manciple's Tale," "The Friar's Tale," and "The Squire's Tale;" and Miss Barrett modernized "Queen Annelida and False Arcite," and "The Complaint of Annelida." The remainder of the volume comprised the "Life of Chaucer," by Dr. Leonard Schmitz; Eulogies on

Chaucer, by his contemporaries, and a sonnet by Charles Wells, author of "Joseph and his Brethren;" and the modernizations and other work, by the Editor and by Robert Bell.

The poem selected by Miss Barrett presented one peculiar feature, being the first of its kind, systematically carried out, that is to be found in English Poetry. Generally, the lady adhered to the principle laid down; but the peculiarity alluded to is to be found in two stanzas only of the present poem, which we will first give in the original, so that readers may judge how the work has been performed.

THE COMPLAINTE OF ANNE-LIDA TO FALSE ARCITE.

VII.

But for J was so plaine to The Arcite,
In all my wordes and workis moche and
    lite,
And was so besy aye you to delite,
    Myne honour only save meke, kind, and fre,
    Therfore Arcite ye put in me this wite,
    Alas? Alas? ye reckin not a mite
    Though that the percing swerde of sorow
        byte
      My woful hert, thorough your cruilte.

VIII.

My swete foe, why do ye so for shame?
And thinkin ye that furthered be your name
    To lovin a newe, and ben untrewe aye,
And putin you in slaundir nowe and blame,
And so to me adversyte and graine,
    That love you most, God thou wotist al-
      waye.
    Yet turne ayen, and yet be plaine some
      daye,

Ant then shall this that now is mis ben
        game,
And al forgevin, whilis J lyve maye.

The following are the modernized ver-
sions of Miss Barrett :—

Stanza VII.

Because I was so plain, Arcite,
 In all my doings, your delight
 Seeking in all things, where I might
In honour,—meek and kind and free;
 Therefore you do me such despite.
Alas! howe'er through cruelty
 My heart with sorrow's sword you smite,
You cannot kill its love.—Ah me!

VIII.

Ah, my sweet foe, why do you so
                For shame?
Think you that praise, in sooth, will raise
                Your name,
Loving anew, and being untrue
                For aye?
Thus casting down your manhood's crown
                In blame,
And working *me* adversity,
                The same,

Who loves you most—(O God thou know'st!)
Alway?
Yet turn again—be fair and plain
Some day;
And then shall this, that seems amiss,
Be game,
All being forgiv'n, while yet from heav'n
I stay.

It will have been perceived that in Miss Barrett's stanza viii. the rhymes are concealed as in the body of the original, both being in the ten-syllable measure in which Chaucer has written the greater part of the poem.

VII.

The longe night this wondir syght I drie,
That on the day, for soche Affray I dye,
  And of al this right naught iwys ye retche,
Ne nevirmoe myne eyin two ben drye,
And to your routhe, and to your trouthe I crye,
  But wel away! to ferre ben they to fetche,
    Thus holdeth me my destiny a wretche,
But me to rede out of this drede or gye
Ne may my wit (so weke is it) not stretche.

Miss Barrett, in her modernization of this, adopted the same arrangement of the rhymes as in stanza viii. Some persons rather blamed her for so doing, and wrongly; for she might, with equal justification, have arranged them in the following order, showing how "cunning an artificer" was the "Father of English Poetry," who is fancied to be rough and crude by those who do not know him.

STANZA XV.

Through the long night
This wondrous sight,
 Bear I,
Which haunted still
The daylight, till
 I die;
But nought of this,
Your heart, I wis,
 Can reach.
Mine eyes down pour,
They never more
 Are dry,

While to your ruth,
And eke your truth,
    I cry—
But, weladay,
Too far be they
    To fetch.
Thus destiny
Is holding me—
    Ah, wretch !
And when I fain
Would break the chain
    And try—
Faileth my wit
(So weak is it)
    With speech.

The following is the first letter I can
find on this subject, evidently written
after receiving proofs of some portion of
the book.

XXI.   [Postmark—Torquay]
                         Dec. 17th, 1840.

"I did not say half enough about the
'Introduction.' The apotheosis of Chaucer, or rather your witness to his poetic

devoutness, is very beautiful,—and that passage, for instance, about the greenness of his green leaves, and the whiteness of his daisies (so true, that is!), and above all, a noble paragraph close to the end, testifying to the devotional verity of every veritable poet. I have read it again and again.

"Notwithstanding all the merit and the grace, do not some of the poems militate against the principle you set out with? I venture to think that the re-fashioners stand—some of them, and in a measure—too far from Chaucer's side—however graceful the attitude. You, yourself, and Wordsworth are most devoutly near. *Most* of the contributors are so, but not all, for even Mr. Leigh Hunt is sometimes satisfied with being with Chaucer in the spirit, and spurns the accidents of body. But Mr. Bell's 'Mars and Venus' is too

smooth and varnished, and redolent of
the nineteenth century, as appears to me,
for spirit *or* body. I think people will
say, you might 'keep more Chaucer.'
But, however, they mayn't; and if they
are not (say what they please) delighted
with this volume, this breathing of sweet
souths over the bank of deathless violets,
there can be no room for delight in their
souls.

"Papa has been to leave his card upon
you, as he tells me. He is a very bad
visitor, or would have done it long ago—
with his strong impression of all your
kindness towards one of his family. Do
go and see them in Wimpole Street, dear
Mr. Horne, some day when you are in
the neighbourhood—before I am there—
if really it is not out of all order in me to
say such a thing. But it would give
them such real pleasure to know you, I

am very sure; and, besides, I shall like
to think that they do.

               " Very truly yours,

                         "E. B. B.

" No, we don't agree; and I want to
set up, not the contrariety, but the
identity of the principle of Greek versification and ours."

The postscript alludes to our projected
lyrical drama of " Psyche."

One of the printer's proofs of part of
my work—all of which I sent to Miss
Barrett and to Leigh Hunt, asking for
their comments and proposed revisions,
in the same way that I had given mine
upon theirs—may afford a slight notion
of the literary, philological, and archæo-
logical queries and contests that attended
this very proper process.   Here are a few
of the marginal and foot-notes.

R. H. " Love will not be constrained by mastery.
  When mastery cometh, the God of Love, anon
  Beateth his wings—and, farewell! he is gone."
E. B. In the second line " comes," says Chaucer, and
  more smoothly.
R. H. Yes, more smoothly, but not so Chaucerian in
  its variety of rhythm. Does your copy print it
  " comes " ? What edition have you ? Mine
  reads " cometh."

The above is a celebrated passage
which has been copied, paraphrastically,
by Pope, and others, without acknow-
ledgment. To continue :—

R. H. " After a time there must be temperance
  In every man that knows self-governance."
E. B. B. I don't think it means self-governance, but
  governance generally. If so, " that knoweth
  governance " would be right.
R. H. " His presence aye desiring, so distraineth,"
E. B. B. Why not,
  " The yearning for his presence so constraineth,"
R. H. Yes, far better.
R. H. " Progressively, as know ye every one,
  Men may engrave and work upon a stone

Till that some figure there imprinted be ;
    So long her friends have soothed her heart," etc.

E. B. B. "Men may engrave so *long* upon a stone,"
    etc.   Shouldn't it suit the other clause ?

R. H. Yes, no doubt.

R. H. " Or else the sorrow had her heart yslain."

E. B. B. Dare you say "yslain" ?   Why not,—
    " Thro' sorrow had her heart been slain."

R. H. Yes, more prudently, and perhaps as good.

R. H. The odour of flowers and freshness of the
    night
    Would any heart have filled and made it
    light,
    That ever was born," etc.

E. B. B. Is it not rough ?

R. H. No, it is Chaucer's harmonious wavy lift and
    roll, as explained in the "Introduction."   It
    would of course be unwieldy if tried by Pope's
    regular finger-scanning by syllables, instead
    of Chaucer's *beats* of time.

R. H. "And home all wend with ease, and full of
    glee,
    Save wretched Aurelius—none was sad but
    he."

E. B. B. Rough—is it not ?

R. H. No ; it is Chaucer's lifting rhythm.   And if it
    were rough, I should retain it for its "wretched"
    effect.

R. H. " Your blissful sister, Lucina the sheen," etc.

E. B. B. Qy. the " Lucina."   Don't you adjust Chaucer's bad quantities ?

R. H. I left that, and others in the proofs, to see what you and Leigh Hunt would say. I suppose we must alter false quantities. Would Landor retain them, black latter and all ?

R. H. " His brother weepeth and waileth privately.'

E. B. B. The metre would be freer without the " and," I think.

R. H. *Stet* the " and," for Chaucerian reasons previously given. The same with regard to several others you have marked.

R. H. " But that a clerk should do a gentle deed
As well as any wight of whom we read."

E. B. B. Doesn't Chaucer mean as well as *either* of *you*—knight or squire ?
" But that a clerk a noble deed should do
Is certain sooth, as well as either of you."

R. H. Yes, you are right; and I like the Chaucerian rhythm of your second line at the close; " as well as ĕither-ŏf-yōu," I propose to alter thus—
" But that a clerk a gentle deed should do
As well—ne'er doubt it—as this knight or you."

R. H. " For, Sir, I will not take a penny of thee

> For all my craft, nor aught for my travaille :
> Thou hast sufficient paid by my vitaille."

E. B. B. I hate and detest those words. Chaucer wouldn't use them *now*. Now, would he ? Besides, I doubt the meaning given to the latter line being quite the right one. How impertinent ! but this is *colophon* to the whole. I fancy something of this sort,—

> "For all my craft, and all my labour given :
> For hospitality, we two are even."

R. H. Sorry to give up the two old words of the original ; but I adopt your suggestion.

E. B. B. Last line of all stands thus in my black letter,—

> "He took his horse, and rode forth on his way."

R. H. Not so in mine. What is the date of yours— and its pedigree ?

These selections from the marginalia on the proofs of a single tale, modernized by the Editor, may give some faint conception of what occurred when Leigh Hunt dealt with my proofs, and I with his. By his seniority in years and literary experience, in addition to his early studies of Chaucer and critical essays, I was prepared for abundant difficulties; but it will be seen how all these were increased when he announced—after we had all commenced upon the plan of as close a literal reading as was compatible with poetical as well as metrical requirements—that he was quite opposed to our leading principle. He announced this, in returning the proofs of my version of the "Prologue to the Canterbury Tales," crowded with revisions on the opposite theory. Of course I accepted as much as I could without violating my own ideas of truthfulness; and I am quite prepared to admit that in all difficult or doubtful passages, a rendering in the spirit would probably be far superior to adhering to the letter. The door, however, Leigh Hunt proposed to open would let in "black spirits and white,"

true spirits and false ; and in dealing with
a great author, it is right to be on the
safe side. The translations of Shelley
from the Greek, Italian, German, and
Spanish, seem to me as near to perfection
as possible. These are in many parts
as fine as their originals ; and with respect to his translations from Goethe's
"Walpurgis Nacht," and " El Magico Pro-
digioso " of Calderon, I consider them not
only faithful, but finer than the originals.
The same method was not so fitting in
Leigh Hunt ; and it would be fitting
to very few. Shelley was a great poet,
and not unlike Calderon, in several
characteristics ;—Leigh Hunt, though an
elegant and delightful poet, was not a
great poet, and not at all like Chaucer..
As to the principle at issue, the close
literal translations of John Oxenford from
Calderon seem to me very preferable to

the fancies many a gentleman might indulge in, and call it the "spirit" of that poet (because it was his own spirit); while the nearest combination of the poetical with the all-but literal, in the present day, is to be found in Denis Florence MacCarthy's translations from the Spanish, even though he does this "in the metres of the original." Still they do not approach what Shelley has done. To return to Leigh Hunt, the opinion of Miss Barrett as to his renderings of Chaucer seems to me quite correct; and most gracefully as he did his part in the "Chaucer Modernized," I prefer what was done by Wordsworth and Miss Barrett, with the understanding that the poems they selected would not be so interesting in themselves, to most people, as those selected by Leigh Hunt.

The subject of rhymes generally is

reserved for a future section, but I may mention here in connection with Leigh Hunt that so strong is the force of habit, that he, with all his long poetical experience, upon coming to a couplet where the words *arch* and *porch* were given as allowable rhymes—as they are, and *must* be, with all of similar family,—wrote in the margin that they were "most impossible," and proposed to substitute the following—

"A Serjeant of the Law, wary and wise,
  Whose robes had often brushed Paul's Paradise,"
    etc.

Passing over the glaring paraphrase, as there is not one word of the second line in Chaucer, the ear that would not admit *arch* and *porch*, can yet give *paradise* and *wise*, not perceiving that the *s* in the latter word is pronounced as *z*—

not *wice*, but *wize*—and takes rank with the allowable rhymes, like all of that class, as well as that of the "arch" and "porch."

Before closing this section the reader may be interested to learn that my first acquaintance with the genial, hospitable, and ever-kindly Robert Bell (author of "A History of Russia," editor of the "Annotated Edition of the English Poets," and for many years editor of the *Home News*), was made through Leigh Hunt, with a view to his co-operation in "Chaucer Modernized." All the contributors, previously named, were highly qualified for the undertaking, and all laboured at it with minute care and thoughtful skill. Yet in consequence of the principle proposed by the editor, and accepted by all, the contest no less than the labour of love entailed upon the editor by the philological enthusiasts, and sincere as well as learned admirers of the Father of English Poetry, far exceeded, in the converse sense, his most sanguine expectations. Whatever alterations were suggested, queries made, or comparison of the texts of different editions proposed, the majority of them were fought out by letters, or marginal and foot-notes all over the proofs. Some of these proofs have been given, and may be considered curiosities of literature. Even when a proposed, or suggested alteration, if only of a single word, was finally accepted, it was seldom without a preliminary contest showing the admirable earnestness of the great poet's translators—but nevertheless trying for the unfortunate one who felt it his duty to tempt his fate on all due, or doubtful, occasions. As a further illustration, here are a few scraps taken from a

single note by Robert Bell, who modernized Chaucer's poem of "The Complaint
of Mars and Venus."

"MY DEAR HORNE,—I send you both
proofs. My reason for asking for a clean
proof was to avoid the danger of confusing
the printers by the numerous marks and
references. . . . . I have adopted the
greater part of your alterations. Wher-
ever I have differed from you, it is upon
mature consideration and after a due
balancing of arguments on both sides.
Your 'sunrise,' in v. 1, although close
to the 'sun uprist,' is not (I think), on
the whole, so close a reflection of his
meaning as my own line, in which the
word 'upland' gives us the picture complete. Besides, 'sun' comes immediately
after. In verse 7, I stand up for 'volup-
tuous joys.' Pray let it remain. In verse

8, 'loving compact' is not so close to the original 'steven,' which literally means an appointment, or 'assignation;' besides, assignation is familiar. But if, on consideration, you prefer the *compact*, you have my assent to its adoption. . . . Verse 17: 'Corse' means, in one sense, body—but in another, 'course,' which is, in my opinion, obviously the meaning here. *Avoiding* the light by baffling turns, creeping and running in the shade, is in all respects better, in my opinion. I should be sorry to lose this. . . .

" Verse 22: *Make* is not intended for 'being.' By examining the other passages in which the singing bird uses it, you will find it means *mate*. I am tolerably certain that my translation is correct, and I think it more poetical.

'This is no feignèd matter that I tell,
My lady is the very spring and well

> Of beauty, gentleness, and liberty :
> Her rich array, a costly *miracle*,' etc.
>
> *Mars,* v. 8.

" Oh ! leave the ' miracle,' v. 5. I must plead also for the restoration of the original line, v. 9. I have brought in the morn in Chaucer's own words. Thanks for calling my attention to this. *L'Envoye:* You are right about ' Granson ' [not grandson]. I am sorry you do not print the stanzas with the indented lines. I have restored a full spelling in those cases where the final syllable is not pronounced. I am afraid I have given you a world of trouble, but I have saved you as much as I could in my proof, which is now completely ready to be printed Mrs. B. read your ' Reve's Tale,' and is decidedly of opinion that there is no objection to it. . . . I must see you soon to settle about the next volume. Ever yours,

" R. B."

And all this, with much more omitted, after Bell had set out with the pleasing but too delusive amenity, that he "had adopted" the greater part of the proposed alterations.

At this period Robert Bell was living in a fine old-fashioned house, with a large garden, some six miles out of London, and gave a cordial standing invitation to his friends to dine there on Sundays. The most frequent guests, that is, once every month or two, were Thackeray, Samuel Lover, Laman Blanchard, Douglas Jerrold, Dr. Mayo, Felix Mendelssohn (when in London), Frank Stone, "Father Prout," and several artists and authors whose names I do not remember; occasionally also, William and Mary Howitt, Dion Boucicault, Dr. Southwood Smith, Leigh Hunt, and Mrs. Jameson.

"Are you a writer of 'moods'?" said

Bell one day to Thackeray. " Yes, as-
suredly," was the answer; " and often
not in the best moods." "Then, sometimes you can't write at all?" "Of
course not; or not fit to be read." "That's
strange," said Bell. " Now, I can take
out my watch—lay it down upon the
table—and write, within a line or two,
the same quantity in the same given
time."

Thackeray was a frequent visitor at
the old garden-mansion when Bell lived
there, and would go on pleasantly for
hours, talking and making sketches in
an album. Some of these were richly
humorous, and accompanied by scraps
of prose or verse. This was before
Thackeray had published " Vanity Fair,"
which at once raised him to his well-
deserved eminence. He himself has re-
lated how this masterpiece of modern

novel-writing was refused in the first instance, both by magazines and as a substantive work; but it was reserved for Mr. Charles Kent's " Footprints on the Road " to make it more recently known that he had also offered himself as an artist, to furnish sketches as illustrations for a popular author's stories, which had been very promptly declined. Bell used to take the utmost delight in seeing him make these fanciful sketches. The drawing-room was very large, and in winter there was a great log-fire. It chanced on a certain evening that the lamp suddenly went out, so that the back part of the room was thrown into shadow; and there stood those huge figures—one upwards of six feet two, and bulky in proportion,—the other (Bell) being at least six feet four, stalwart and gaunt—with the large log-fire at steady red heat in front of them, and their great shoulders and backs in dark shade. It suggested to the imagination a scene of giants in a forest, holding high conference, or of the meeting between the Chancellor, " tower-heavy Turketul," and " Gorm " the Scandinavian sea-king, in the fine Chronicle play of " Athelstan." What a pity that Bell's amiable, and not unfrequently " inspired " visitor, Mendelssohn, did not chance to be at the pianoforte that evening ! He would certainly have improvised some wonderful symphony on the occasion.

III.

"A New Spirit of the Age."

III.

"A NEW SPIRIT OF THE AGE."

TO be anonymous is to be safe, and the
pseudonymous is almost equally so,
even if the individual be pretty clearly
known in either case ; but the moment
an author gives his name openly to a free
examination of living men and their
doings, he walks into circling fields of
battle, abounding in martello towers,
ambuscades, and secret rifle-pits, the
marksmen in which will sometimes be-
queath a weapon to their sons and their
surviving friends. That this is so, the
experience of all those who have placed

themselves in such a position attests;
but why it should be so, while the anonymous critic always remains unassailed,
even when his identity is ascertained,
would take too much time to discuss.
We may simply assume that the offend-
ing opinions being apparently impersonal,
the wound to the offended parties is less
painful to human self-love. In all cases,
however, the critic is bound to adopt
the best means in his power to be right,
and take his chance for all that may
follow.

To any author or editor, about to publish a book in which there will inevitably
be many things affecting contemporaries,
the most valuable friend and counsellor
he can have will be one who, possessing
a finely suitable intellect for the matter
in question, and having gathered together
the requisite knowledge, is dwelling com-

paratively out of the world and its con-
flicting people and opinions, yet taking a
deep interest in the best things that are
going on, coupled with a due indignation
at the worst, and who has magnanimity
to admire, as well as moral courage to
demur or denounce, ever holding within,
as at a shrine, an unmixed love and spirit
of truth. Such a friend and counsellor,
on a certain occasion, I had in Miss
Barrett.

Soon after the completion of "Chaucer
Modernized," two volumes of literary
criticism, under the title of "A New
Spirit of the Age," were projected. As
in the former case, the work was to be
edited and partly written by myself, and
the principal and most valuable of my coadjutors was Miss Barrett. As the second
edition of the book has been out of print
for thirty years in England (though I am

aware that at least three " unauthorised "
editions were subsequently printed in
America) and the authorship, whether
single-handed or combined, of the various
critiques, has never hitherto been divulged
—the editor agreeing to " stand fire " for
everything—I think the " key," which
I can supply, may not be without considerable literary interest. I may now
say, for instance, that the critique entitled " William Wordsworth and Leigh
Hunt " (two authors and men of the most
unlike kind being purposely contrasted,
in order to bring out their great merits,
with some few defects in each, the more
forcibly from juxtaposition) was written
in about equal proportions by Miss Barrett and myself. This was done at first
in separate manuscripts, and then each
interpolated the work of the other " as
the spirit moved." It was written in

letters, now and then of considerable length.

I believe I am making public for the first time the fact that the mottoes, which are singularly happy and appropriate, were for the most part supplied by Miss Barrett and Robert Browning, then unknown to each other. What could be better for Tennyson than the line from Carlyle?—

" Touches there are, be the heavens ever thanked, of
    new Sphere melody."

Or more delicately suggestive of ironical approval than the lines chosen for Sir Henry Taylor, from Akenside—

" Hand in hand at Wisdom's shrine,
    Beauty with Truth I strive to join,
    And grave Assent with glad Applause;
      .To paint the story of the soul,
      And Plato's vision to control
By Verulamian laws ! "

And these from Donne (Elegy A)—

" But as we, in our isle imprisoned,
   Where cattle only, and divers dogs are bred,
   The precious unicorns, strange monsters call,—
   So thought he sweets strange, that had none at all."

Or more strikingly characteristic for the author of " Lays of Ancient Rome " than

" Arma, virumque cano "—

or these on Landor—

" Thy worth and skill exempts thee from the throng."
                                          Milton.

                  " Let his page
   Which charms the chosen Spirits of the Age,
   Fold itself up for a serener clime
   Of years to come, and find its recompense
   In that just expectation."
                                          Shelley.

The review of the writings of Walter Savage Landor (certainly one of the best in the book) was mainly written by Miss

Barrett. It was forwarded in two letters, which were carefully transcribed. What she had done was preceded by a few biographical and other remarks, founded upon communications forwarded to me by Mr. Landor. The spirit of a Greek epigram written by him on Napoleon the First, will be understood by the following interesting episode in the author's private history :—

XXII.

"Mr. Landor went to Paris in the beginning of the century, where he witnessed the ceremony of Napoleon being made Consul for life, amidst the acclamations of multitudes. He subsequently saw the dethroned and deserted Emperor pass through Tours, on his way to embark, as he intended, for America. Napoleon was attended only by a single servant,

and descended at the Prefecture, unrecog-
nised by anybody except Landor. The
people of Tours were most hostile to
Napoleon; as a republican politician,
Landor had always felt a hatred towards
him, and now he had but to point one
finger at him, and it would have done
what all the artillery and 'infernal
machines' of twenty years of wars and
passions had failed to do. The people
would have torn him to pieces. Need it
be said that Landor was too 'good a
hater,' and too noble a man to avail himself of such an opportunity. He held his
breath, and let the hero pass. Perhaps
after all there was no need of any of this
hatred on the part of Landor, who, in
common with many other excessively
self-willed men, was as much exasperated
at Napoleon's commanding successes, as
at his falling off from pure republican

principles.   Howbeit, Landor's great
hatred, and yet 'greater' forbearance,
are hereby recorded. ''*

Miss Barrett's letter proceeded thus :—

"In the case of Mr. Landor, however,
other causes than the originality of his
faculty opposed his favour with the public.
He has the most select audience, perhaps
—the fittest, the fewest—of any distinguished author of the day ; and this
of his choice.   'Give me,' he said in
one of his prefaces, 'ten accomplished
men for readers, and I am content.' †
And the event does not by any means,

* "A New Spirit of the Age," Vol. i., pp. 161-2 ;
second edition, 1844.

† In reply to an adverse criticism in a certain quarterly journal, he offered the critic "three hot penny
rolls " for his luncheon, if he could write anything as
good.   This was not exactly the way to make friends
with the tribe.

so far as we could desire, outstrip the
modesty, or despair, or disdain, of this
aspiration.

" He writes criticism for critics, and
poetry for poets ; his drama, when he is
dramatic, will suppose neither pit nor
gallery, nor critics, nor laws. He is not
a publican among poets—he does not sell
his Amreeta cups upon the highway. He
delivers them rather with the dignity of
a giver to ticketed persons ; analysing
their flavour and fragrance with a learned
delicacy, and an appeal to the esoteric.
His very spelling of English is uncommon
and theoretic ; and as if poetry were not,
in English, a sufficiently unpopular dead
language, he has had recourse to writing
poetry in Latin ; with dissertations on
the Latin tongue, to fence it out doubly
from the populace. *Odi profanum vulgus
et arceo.*

"Mr. Landor is classical in the highest sense. His conceptions stand out clearly cut and fine, in a magnitude and nobility as far as possible removed from the small and sickly vagueness common to this century of letters. If he seems obscure at times it is from no infirmity or inadequacy of thought or word, but from extreme concentration and involution in brevity; for a short string can be tied in a knot as well as a long one. He can be tender, as the strong can best be; and his pathos, when it comes, is profound. His descriptions are full and startling; his thoughts self-produced and bold; and he has the art of taking a common-place under a new aspect, and of leaving the Roman brick, marble. In marble, indeed, he seems to work; for there is an angularity in the workmanship, whether of prose or verse, which the very exquisiteness of the

polish renders more conspicuous. You
may complain, too, of hearing the chisel;
but after all you applaud the work—it is
a work well done. The elaboration produces no sense of heaviness; the severity
of the outline does not militate against
beauty; if it is cold, it is also noble; if
not impulsive, it is suggestive. As a
writer of Latin poems he ranks with our
most successful scholars and poets;
having less harmony and majesty than
Milton had—when he aspired to that
species of 'Life in Death'—but more
variety and freedom of utterance. Mr.
Landor's English prose writings possess
most of the characteristics of his poetry,
only they are more perfect in their class.
His 'Pericles and Aspasia' and 'Pen-
tameron' are books for the world and for
all time, whenever the world and time
shall come to their senses about them;

complete in beauty of sentiment and subtlety of criticism. His general style is highly scholastic and elegant; his sentences have *articulations*, if such an expression may be permitted, of very excellent proportions. And, abounding in striking images and thoughts, he is remarkable for making clear ground there, and for lifting them, like statues to pedestals, where they may be seen most distinctly, and strike with the most enduring, though often the most gradual, impression. This is the case both in his prose works and his poetry. It is more conspicuously true of some of his smaller poems, which for quiet classic grace and tenderness, and exquisite care in their polish, may best be compared with beautiful cameos and vases of the antique."

Two of Landor's works are probably

known to less than half-a-dozen people of the present day. One is entitled "Poems from the Arabic and Persian." They are as full of ornate fancy, grace, and tenderness, as the originals from which they appeared to be translated, and were accompanied by a number of erudite critical notes, likely to cause much searching among Oriental scholars. And the search, after all, was certain to be in vain, as no such poems really existed in the Arabic or Persian. The other *brochure* was "A Satire upon Satirists," a scathing piece of heroic verse—a copy of which Mr. Landor sent to me.

The following letters form an amusing contrast to the preceding, and are valuable as illustrations of the "lighter moods" that relieved the tedium of Miss Barrett's enforced seclusion :—

XXIII. [No date.]

" Ah, my dear Mr. Horne, you will conclude—(for you may conclude, though I cannot!) you will conclude from certain facts that I am very like a *broom!* —not Lord Brougham, who only does a *little* of everything;—and not a wheeled brougham, which will stop when it is bidden;—and not a new broom, which sweeps clean and then has done with it; but that bewitched broom in the story, which, being sent to draw water, drew bucket after bucket, until the whole house was in a flood. Montaigne says somewhere that to stop gracefully is a sure proof of high race in a horse. I wonder what not to stop at all is proof of—in horse, man, or woman? After all, I am not improving my case by this additional loquacity; and the case is bad enough, perhaps—viz., that you asked

me to write four or five pages for your
work, and that I have written what you
see! Well, take the sheets—I make you
a present of them to cut into pieces,—
abbreviate in any possible way, or put
into the fire altogether, should your judgment suggest that stronger measure.
Indeed, I did not mean to write so much
—I didn't think of writing your whole
book for you!

"Oh, of course! You are free to interpolate as well as to cut down. In fact
the papers are as much yours as if you
had written them; and I sign over my
personality in them to you herewith.
Would it were better worth the having!

"Ever truly yours,

"E. B. B."

XXIV.   October 2, 1843. Friday.

"Thank you, my dear Mr. Horne—I am

glad to be excused the political economy. Yet if I had done it, I had *done* it—and you would have probably had some exceedingly 'original views'—something to make the economists stare wonderfully and think of a new era. Being out of my depth I should certainly be profound. You would have had to go to Mr. W. J. Fox to know what I meant, and Mr. Fox couldn't have told you—for I should have had this in common with Jeremy Bentham that it would be necessary for somebody to translate me. Well!— you see what you have lost, in 'my great large hand.' Ah, but (as you said to me about the portrait) if you repent you can't have it otherwise now. You have done for yourself—and I close with the proposition about Wordsworth and Hunt.

"In respect to Miss Mitford, you and I were talking collaterally, and should as

soon have come together as parallel lines.
You thought I was praying for the introduction of her portrait, whereas I never
thought of the engravings, but of the
literature, — my impression being that
you meant to pass her over 'in solemn
silence,' as defunct. Since you mention
her honourably, we are at one,—and I
admit at once that her portrait being
before the public in various degrees of
likeness, any additional expense *on that
head* would be superfluous. You mention
her—and it is enough—and in mentioning
you must not superannuate her. She is
not very much above fifty—looking older
than her actual age—and has a far better
right to a place in the book, according to
the principle of the book, than the Camp-
bells, Rogers, Wordsworths, etc. As to
the question you put to me, her 'Belford
Regis' should probably take rank as her

best work; it has most power and most character; and is somewhat less uniformly soft and green than 'Our Village' is. The 'Village,' however, is, by association, my favourite. If read by snatches, it comes on the mind as the summer air and the sweet hum of rural sounds would float upon the senses through an open window in the country, and leaves with you for the whole day a tradition of fragrance and dew. Both works are composites of separate papers—and the only unity (except, indeed, that of place) is in the cordial and cheerful spirit of the writer. She is in fact a sort of prose Crabbe in the sun, but with more grace and less strength; and also with a more steadfast look upon scenic nature—never going higher than the earth to look for the beautiful, but always finding it as surely as if we went higher. She is 'matter-of-fact,' she says, which may be so, but then she idealizes matter of fact before she touches it, and thus her matter of fact is as beautiful as the matter of phantasy of other people. Who would not go and gather Lilies of the Valley with her from the Silchester woods. Indeed if the world were as she paints it, we should all choose to live out of doors, and nobody catch any cold! Her last work (except the prose in Finden) is 'Country Stories,' a sort of codicil to 'The Village' and 'Belford Regis,' and she did begin a novel, which I am afraid, from the long loiterings, will never be ended. Her 'Dramatic Scenes' you probably know, as well as her Tragedies. In my own mind—and Mr. Kenyon agrees with me —she herself is better and stronger than any of her books; and her letters and con-

versation show more grasp of intellect
and general power than would be infer-
able from her finished compositions. I
do not know whether you are of our
opinion. In her works, however, through
all the beauty there is a clear vein of
sense, and a quickness of observation
which takes the character of a refined
shrewdness. Do you not think so?
And is she not besides most intensely a
woman, and an Englishwoman? Very
well! I will be good as I am fair—*i.e.*,
by courtesy. And I will be very courteous
to your right honourable printers, who
can't be at the trouble to turn over a leaf
or read from anything except large paper,
and an inch of margin on each side!
Very well, they shall have their will—
although, to be sure, I have been in the
habit of writing for the press on the
ordinary long note paper, and on both

sides the page, and never heard a printer's murmur. And thank you for your praise. Always welcome, be sure. 'And for the trust you put in me.

"And so 'in confidence deep as the grave,'

"Ever yours,

"E. B. B.

"'How I do go on in the dark!' To be sure I do. The dark, you know, is my particular province—even *without* the political economy. *That* would have made me a Princess of Darkness. Surely, by the way, Mr. Chorley's book was after 1833. I never remember dates, but surely it was."

A very neat and characteristic pen-and-ink portion of little "Flush"—humorously made rather like herself — was placed at the opening of Miss Barrett's

next letter, evidently written in reply to
my request for some biographical facts to
be made use òf in the article on herself.
Unfortunately they reached me too late
to prevent some errors which crept in.

XXV.   " October 5th, 1843.

" Here I send you one of the ' Spirits
of the Age,' strongly recommending it to
a place on your frontispiece. It is Flush's
portrait, I need scarcely say; and only fails
of being an excellent substitute for mine
through being more worthy than I can
be counted.

" Ah, my dear Mr. Horne, your application made me smile—a little with
pleasure and pride that you should think
of ' illustrating ' your book with my darkness, and a little with self-mockery at
the idea of it. No, no, no,—to ' recline '
for any set of publishers in the world,

even for yours, surpasseth the vanity that
is in me. You know Mrs. B—— told
you that I was 'modest,' and neither you
nor I would believe a word of it; and
here is the first proof that either of us ever
had of it—unless (which is my opinion)
it prove to be an instinct of self-preserva-
tion instead. The last time I 'reclined'
for my picture was for a miniature by Mrs.
Carter, just before I left Devonshire; and
I did it for love's sake and papa's. And
yet, although she was so obliging as to
paint a very pretty little girl with unex-
ceptionable regularity of features, he was
ungrateful enough to throw it down
with a pshaw! and deny the likeness altogether. There is no portrait of me at
all which is considered like—except one
painted in my infancy, where I appear
in the character of a fugitive angel, which
papa swears by all his gods is very like

me to this day, and which perhaps may
be like—about the wings. In conclusion,
you see, I both can't and won't send you
a picture for such a purpose—it is a super-
fluity of negation ! ' Won't,' would have
done very well for a woman—now would
it not ? ' Beseech your grace ' do not
be angry with me. It seems to me an
ultra-impossibility to send my portrait
to a publisher for introduction to the
public—and not even to please

' The great Orion sloping slowly to the west '

could I bring my mind to such
a thing. It may be affectation—who
knows ? And yet really I think it is
too impulsive, instinctive, and single-
thoughted to be affectation, even under
that thickest of disguises which is assumed by our own motives before our
own eyes.

" Since I am beginning to be philoso-
phical we might as well pass suddenly
to the 'Biographical Sketch.' So you
think that I am in the habit of keeping
biographical sketches in my table-drawer
for the use of hypothetical editors ?
Alas !—

" Once, indeed, for one year, I kept
a diary in detail and largely; and at the
end of the twelve months was in such
a crisis of self-disgust that there was
nothing for me but to leave off the diary.
Did you ever try the effect of a diary
upon your own mind ? It is curious,
especially where elastic spirits and
fancies are at work upon a fixity of
character and situation. You see how
it is. I have no biographical sketch, and
perhaps if I had——My dear Mr. Horne,
the public do not care for me enough to
care at all for my biography. If you say

anything of me (and I am not affected
enough to pretend to wish you to be
absolutely silent, if you see any occasion
to speak), it must be as a writer of rhymes,
and not as the heroine of a biography.
You must not allow your kindness for me
to place me in a prominency which I
have to deserve—and do not yet deserve.
And then as to stories, my story amounts
to the knife-grinder's, with nothing at all
for a catastrophe. A bird in a cage
would have as good a story. Most of
my events, and nearly all my intense
pleasures, have passed in my *thoughts*.
I wrote verses—as I dare say many have
done who never wrote any poems—very
early; at eight years old and earlier.
But, what is less common, the early fancy
turned into a will, and remained with me,
and from that day to this, poetry has
been a distinct object with me — an

object to read, think, and live for. And
I could make you laugh, although you
could not make the public laugh, by the
narrative of nascent odes, epics, and
didactics crying aloud on obsolete Muses
from childish lips. The Greeks were my
demi-gods, and haunted me out of Pope's
Homer until I dreamt more of Aga-
memnon than of Moses the black pony.
And thus my great 'epic' of eleven or
twelve years old, in four books, and
called 'The Battle of Marathon,' and of
which fifty copies were printed because
papa was bent upon spoiling me—is
Pope's Homer done over again, or rather
undone; for, although a curious production for a child, it gives evidence only
of an imitative faculty and an ear, and
a good deal of reading in a peculiar direction. The love of Pope's Homer threw
me into Pope on one side and into Greek

on the other, and into Latin as a help to Greek—and the influence of all these tendencies is manifest so long afterwards as in my 'Essay on Mind,' a didactic poem written when I was seventeen or eighteen, and long repented of as worthy of all repentance. The poem is imitative in its form, yet is not without traces of an individual thinking and feeling—the bird pecks through the shell in it. With this it has a pertness and pedantry which did not even then belong to the character of the author, and which I regret now more than I do the literary defectiveness.

" All this time, and indeed the greater part of my life, we lived at Hope End, a few miles from Malvern, in a retirement scarcely broken to me except by books and my own thoughts, and it is a beautiful country, and was a retirement happy in many ways, although the very peace of it troubles the heart as it looks back. There I had my fits of Pope, and Byron, and Coleridge, and read Greek as hard under the trees as some of your Oxonians in the Bodleian; gathered visions from Plato and the dramatists, and eat and drank Greek and made my head ache with it. Do you know the Malvern Hills? The hills of Piers Plowman's Visions? They seem to me my native hills; for, although I was born in the county of Durham, I was an infant when I went first into their neighbourhood, and lived there until I had passed twenty by several years. Beautiful, beautiful hills, they are! And yet, not for the whole world's beauty, would I stand in the sunshine and the shadow of them any more. It would be a mockery, like the taking back of a broken flower to its stalk. From thence we went to Sidmouth

for two years; and I published there
my translation of Æschylus, which was
written in twelve days, and should have
been thrown into the fire afterwards,—the
only means of giving it a little warmth.
The next removal was to London, and
brought us close to *you*—did it not? To
74, Gloucester Place, when you were at
75—was it not? I was unaware of it,
however, until papa had purchased this
house, and we were dwellers here. And
then came the failure in my health, which
never had been strong (at fifteen I nearly
died), and the publication of 'The Seraphim,' the only work I care to acknowledge, and then the enforced exile to
Torquay, with prophecy in the fear and
grief and reluctance of it—a dreadful
dream of an exile, which gave a night-
mare to my life for ever, and robbed it
of more than I can speak of here; do

not speak of that anywhere. *Do not speak of that,* dear Mr. Horne; and for the rest, you see that there is nothing to say. It is 'a blank, my lord.' Yet I could write an autobiography, but not now, and not for an indifferent public; of whom, by the way, I never did and do not complain, seeing that they received my 'Seraphim' with some kindness, and that everything published previously by me I reject myself, and cast upon the ground as unworthy. The 'Seraphim' has faults enough—and weaknesses, besides—but my voice is in it, in its individual tones, and not inarticulately.

"Writing, writing, writing I am, yet writing nothing which you ask for. Here at least are the dates of the three books: 'Essay on Mind, and other poems,' 1826; 'Prometheus, and other poems,' 1835; 'The Seraphim, and other poems,' 1838.

My wish, my private wish, is that you should say nothing of the two first books, or sweep them cursorily with the most extreme feather of your wing. The first book especially, consisting of poems from the age of thirteen (of which are several of the smaller ones), and didactic pedantry of almost as absolute an immaturity, certainly has a claim to escape from public criticism. Its circulation has been very limited of its own accord, and my will has contracted it further; for I would as soon circulate a caricature or lampoon on myself as that essay. And for the 'Prometheus,' all the remaining copies are safely locked up in the wardrobe of papa's bedroom, entombed as safely as Œdipus among the olives. A few of the fugitive poems connected with that translation may be worth a little, perhaps; but they have not so much goodness as to overcome the badness of the blasphemy of Æschylus.

"Yes, I have recovered my pet. No, I have 'idealised' none of the dog-stealing. I had no time. I was crying while he was away, and I was accused so loudly of 'silliness' and 'childishness' afterwards, that I was glad to dry my eyes, and forget my misfortunes by way of rescuing my reputation. After all, it was excusable that I cried. Flushie is my friend—my companion—and loves me better than he loves the sunshine without. Oh, and if you had seen him, when he came home and threw himself into my arms, palpitating with joy—in that dumb inarticulate ecstasy which is so affecting —love without speech! 'You had better give your dog something to eat,' said the thief to my brother when he yielded up his prize for a bribe, 'for he has tasted

nothing since he has been with us.' *And*
he had been with them for three days, and
yet his heart was so full when he came
home that he could not eat, but shrank
away from the plate and laid down his
head on my shoulder. The spirit of love
conquered the animal appetite even in
that dog. He is worth loving. Is he
not?

"I shall keep this letter in the hope of
seeing Mr. Kenyon and asking about
Macaulay. You are very right in admir-
ing Macaulay, who has a noble, clear,
metallic note in his soul, and makes us
ready by it for battle. I very much admire Mr. Macaulay, and could scarcely
read his ballads and keep lying down.
They seemed to draw me up to my feet
as the mesmeric powers are said to do.
I do not, however, think that Mr. Kenyon
knows him as intimately as you fancy—

although to be sure Mr. Kenyon knows everybody, more or less.

" And now I put an end to this letter (though you would scarcely suppose it) and wish you all success, prosperity, and laurels in your new field. I thought you had vanished from every field, and that I was not likely to find you higher up than Hades. But being found, may you be successful. You walk in honourable steps, following Hazlitt, and the work is likely to be popular. Are you aware that Mr. Chorley published a work called the 'Authors and Authoresses of England,' some time ago, with profiles and short notices ? When I say some time ago, I mean some years. And your book will probably assume a higher character, and go deeper.

" Ever truly yours,

" E. B. B.

" Mr. Kenyon I have seen, and ascertained that he does not know Macaulay in any degree, less or more."

XXVI.   " Eleven o'Clock a.m., Wednesday.
[Postmark—Nov. 1st, 1843.]

" MY DEAR MR. HORNE,—I write in all the hurry of blots in reply to your note ' by express,' this morning to assure you solemnly that if Mr. Reade really meant to tell you that he was aware of my having touched your work with my little finger, he must have had it from especial revelation of angels. I solemnly assure you that I never mentioned the subject even to my own father, that I have never named ' The Spirit of the Age,' or anything bearing a relation to it, even to Miss Mitford, lest the very suggestion of a surmise should be made or repeated. *You* are in the wrong, be sure, my dear

Mr. Horne. Thus it must have been : that Mr. Reade heard from Miss Mitford, and intended to express to *you*, that I was to be mentioned in the book, and that you mistook his meaning for that of my hand being employed in it. Miss Mitford knew I was to be in it, because she wrote to tell me of the book, with some kind expressions of congratulation that now she should have my picture, etc. To which I replied (the only word I ever said on the subject at all) that you had indeed been good enough to propose it, but that I had declined the honour and crown of the portrait, by an instinct of what was *un*due to me. Now do you see ? I know nothing of Mr. Reade ; and if I did, I have *mentioned the subject to nobody—* not to Miss Mitford—not to Mr. Kenyon. I am innocent,—stand with washed hands before you. In fact, I am the person to be vexed, and I am vexed thoroughly. Oh! will this be in time to *suppress* your notes of explanation? Try to explain away the explanation. I quite see that I ought not to be named in connection with this book, and for several other than the obvious reasons I *object* to being named. It is a service of danger to write in the book, and I, who am a woman, am not made for war. Do what you can to get me out of this scrape. In reply to your letter of yesterday, I will do anything you think me fit for—on conditions of strict secrecy. But how is it to be kept now? I am quite vexed—and yesterday I was pleased by your letter. Mr. Reade! Who would ever have suspected *him* of having special revelations?

"Ever yours,

"E. B. B.

"Are you sure that you said nothing yourself to Miss Mitford? If you did, it is explained."

XXVII.   "November 3rd, 1843.

"I do not hear from you, and am wondering why and how. I am not easy about this Mr. Reade and his secret informations, and at your believing for one moment that I was faithless enough to be capable of sinning against a confidence reposed in me. The absolute impossibility of his speaking to the end you understood, with any grounds for so speaking (unless you yourself gave the tenure of them to him or others), I wish I could make as plain to you as it is to me. It is absolutely impossible. I said to Flush, 'Only *you* could betray me. Are *you* the traitor?' And he looked at me with dilated earnest steady eyes, and then kissed both my hands—as if to assure me of truth and fealty. So as Flush didn't tell, nobody else from this room did. Once, with my living voice, have I named your book, and that was to Mr. Kenyon, when I tried to get the information for you about Macaulay; and *once*, in my correspondence, to Miss Mitford, after she made the observation I told you of in my last note, and to the simple effect I told you. By the way, I hope you could read the last note. I was so vexed and so hurried as I wrote it. And I hope you believed in my absolute innocence as you read it, from the very hurry and vexation, of which the traces must at least have been natural.

"Yesterday I had a letter from Miss Mitford, and I opened it trembling, lest I should read something more of Mr. Reade's informations. No, not a word.

I think I must be right in my suggestion
that you mistook what he meant to refer
to—and that he meant to refer to me—
written about rather than writing. Or
else (which has occurred to me since) he
may have mistaken some expression of
Miss Mitford's (*i.e.*, understood by it
what she did not mean to express) about
my being *in* the work, and have fallen
upon the truth so, by accident. Any way
I am very sorry that you should have
sent him explanations by express, because, you see, Mr. Reade has the habit
of repeating other people's sayings, *beginning with their poetry*, and he is not
likely to stop for us. Besides, men
always *do* talk, don't they? They can't
keep a secret, can they? That is my
remark.

"I had a letter from Mr. Mathews, of
New York, yesterday, with a cancelling of

the dishonour of the editor of *Graham's*, in consequence of which he (Mr. Mathews) says that he has smoothed his brows and sent to that magazine the copy of 'Orion' which I sent for the purpose. He does not, however, say a word about my other proposition. Probably he has not had time, since the quarrel, to enter into another treaty; and I am not myself quite so anxious about it, fearing to draw you into a scrape. Mr. Mathews is delighted with 'Orion,' and is going to send you soon some poems of his own, as homage from the West. He desires me to make known generally that a Copyright Club, for the protection of authors poor and honest, is being established at New York, and that Mr. Bryant is president, and he, Mr. Mathews, secretary, and that we are all to be protected most effectually.

" Write and tell me that you believe
me to be honest. Not 'honest, honest
Iago,' but in a better sense. I am vexed
for myself, vexed for you, and vexed, in
a compound relation, for your thoughts
of me. It is abominable for a person to
be so discreet as I have been, and all in
vain! There is no poetical nor any other
kind of justice in it.

" As to Mr. Reade—but really I am too
cross about him to speak of him.

" A gentleman with whom I am personally unacquainted, sent me a few days
ago a little book which he had written
upon 'predestination.' As you are fond
of 'dogmas,' I will lend it to you. Yesterday I wrote to thank him, and referring to his note for the address, I read
Highlands. Immediately I began to rage
and roar in the spirit about Mr. Reade;
which was very improper, considering

that I had just been writing controversy upon predestination.

"Mr. Merry, by the way, is a man of excellent intuitions, and I have a high esteem for him. Also, I once before had some correspondence with him on the subject of another little work from his hand, called 'A Happy Futurity;' but then it was long ago, and I had quite forgotten since that he lived at *Highlands*.

"Yours faithfully, dear Mr. Horne, and by no means faithlessly,

"E. B. B."

In a previous letter Miss Barrett agreed to my proposal that she should write the paper on "William Wordsworth and Leigh Hunt;" consequently the first draft of the paper on them was written by her, and she forwarded it to me in letters. These I interpolated throughout, sometimes at considerable length. A rough proof of this was then transmitted to Miss Barrett. Very speedily there came to me a letter containing objections and remonstrances with reference to some of my interpolated remarks concerning Leigh Hunt. As to Wordsworth we were fully agreed.

XXVIII.   "November, 1843, Monday.

" Thanks, many and true, my dear Mr. Horne, for the glance at the proofs. You shall find me what is called a 'safe person,' and worthy of confidence; and I am secretly proud of the confidence and the association, and of your condescending to think that we write pretty well together. Reading this paper has amused me beyond your guessing. I have not a copy of my MS. (an evidence of the 'safety'); but I remember nearly all the way, and am particularly amused to observe where, and in what octave, you strike your trumpet-note of accompaniment, and where you see fit to change the key, as choragus. Really the paper, altogether, reads well. And now to my criticism.

" I have been intrepid enough to make some slight alterations and corrections of the proof where there could be no doubt, I fancied, of the truth of my suggestion ; —and in other places I have written down my quære.

" I object to your addition to ' the cheek of the impartial historian '—of ' as of the true critics of present times.' There is confusion and pleonasm, and a division of the identity of impartial historians and true critics. Why not simply ' the cheek of the true critic of present times ' ? It may be one or the other, but shouldn't be both, I think.

" 'Alfred Tennyson.'—It appears to me certain that Tennyson wrote long and long after the extinction—as a critical phrase—of 'the Cockney School.' And even if this were not so, it appears to me doubtful whether Tennyson lived in London long enough to take class as a hypothetical cockney. His family have a country house somewhere in Kent; and civically he never did any more—did he? —than 'visit' London? *That* is my impression, at least.

" Below—I fancy that our 'two heads' [instead of being better than 'one,' as had been suggested] rather knock against each other, in the observation about the imaginations of Wordsworth and Hunt. The sentences straggle, and do not follow according to the laws of what Browne calls 'suggestion.' Look at them and see.

" 'In exterior nature Wordsworth has

a wider faith, *and,* a less discriminating taste.' Why not 'or' instead of 'and'? It is correcter, I think.

" 'In religious feeling, however, he [Leigh Hunt] may have been misrepresented : '—

" And, on the last page—' They were provoked at his tendency to confound the distinctions of good and evil, by saying too much on the amiable side of the condemned.'

" Now, will you have patience with me, my dear Mr. Horne, while I speak a little on these two texts, and regret deeply that you should allow your friendship and admiration for Mr. Leigh Hunt to draw the question away from the truth to the extent of this inch ? ' *Amicus Socrates, sed magis amica veritas,*' is the noblest expression of friendship—surely —and the most , acceptable even to

Socrates. *You*, who are candid—tell me if it is true that he was 'misrepresented' in matters of religion?

" Is it true—strictly true—that he confounded the distinction of good and evil *only* by saying too much and too amiably 'for the condemned'? Does it not stand clear out in his books, in his early writings, that he confounded good and evil, in *principles* rather than by *persons?* If you deny this, you may become a partial historian—but is the *fact* altered, before the eyes of your own friendship?—that fact being so undeniable that the poet himself has taken advantage of the opportunity of a later edition, in order to obliterate and change the offensive passages.*

---

* I do not consider that Leigh Hunt ever obliterated or changed any part of his early writings, *in principle*, but only omitted or softened the same in expression.

" That great injustice has been done to Mr. Leigh Hunt, I am well aware,—that what was reprobated in him passed free in others, I am well aware. But one sort of injustice is not to be corrected by *another*, and on the point of what his views of religious truth and moral virtue used to be, I cannot agree with you that he has been ' misrepresented ; ' and I am of opinion that you confront the offensive injustice of the world with the defensive injustice of your individual friendship.

" For myself, I will say that, out of the circle of Mr. Leigh Hunt's immediate friends, there cannot be one who regards him with more respect and admiration than I do. Yet I must write so.

" Also, it seems to me clear—you have been guilty of some (and that no small degree of) ' offensive ' injustice to the great fathers of our poetry, Chaucer and

Shakspere, by accusing them of confounding, or seeming to confound, the
bounds of good and evil, which they
never did confound ; which, in all their
universality of heart and intellect, and
their boundless charity and sympathy
with human nature, they never did confound—seeing that in this they were god-
like, that they would not consent to lower
from their starry height, to the level of
persons, the *principles* of either verity
or virtue.

" Can you forgive me, my dear friend,
for writing my whole thought out so
freely? As we see truth, it becomes
the duty of each of us to utter it,—
and just in proportion to my high
consideration for you—and, if you will
permit me to say so, my true and
grateful regard for you—was I pricked
and provoked by your line of defence.

The generous motive is obvious, and *therefore* I should like the defence to be *worthy of the motive*. Forgive me, at least, and—try if you can avoid charging our Chaucer and Shakspere (in contrariousness to your own estimate of the former, in the admirable preliminary Essay to the Modernization) of confounding, or seeming to confound, the bounds of good and evil.

"There now! You will never send me any more proof-sheets. Nay, who knows but that you will quarrel with me for life as a climax of vengeance!

Forgive me generously, on the contrary. For I am faithfully your friend, so much the more,

"E. B. B.

"Is Mr. Hunt a voluminous writer? I should have taken quite a contrary view—but ignorantly, perhaps.

" Have I taken a note of my admiration of your estimate (in one respect) of Wordsworth, as *no*-prophet ? It seems to me both subtle and true."

The gracious hand that wrote the foregoing controversial letter can no longer make a rejoinder. I therefore must do no more than plead guilty to having said, directly or by inference, that Leigh Hunt's "boundless charity, and sympathy with human nature," *had* often led him to regard evil acts or conventional crimes in the same extenuating, if not pardoning, spirit that was frequently displayed by Chaucer and Shakspere. But "to the pure, all things are pure," and while the fair controversialist was living, I could not then have quoted (and for the same reasons do not feel I can do it now) a variety of questionable and most unquestionable acts and scenes portrayed vividly by those great poets, which are sometimes "made fun of," and in other cases are "let off" very easily—if not with a smile (*aside*).

Here follows the second letter, mainly on the same subject, after my reply. It commences quite in her "winning way," but very often slants off into her usual vigorous style when excited.

XXIX.   "December, 1848, Wednesday."

" You are kind and generous, and I did you so much dishonour as really to be a little uneasy lest you might be angry with me for what I said !

" After all, my dear Mr. Horne, the reference as it stood would have appeared to many readers, as to myself, directed to both theological and moral points ;—inasmuch as the circumstance of your 'not knowing,' or dismissing from the observation of your soul, certain passages of former works of Hunt, will not alter the relations of them in the memory of other people. They cannot but remember such things ' were '—and it would be painful to you to understand thoroughly how in some quarters, some recollections are ' at top' of the beauty and glory. Strictly in confidence [all three then living ;—all three now dead], and to prove to you that all this is not a dream of mine, and how high certain influences can splash—I will name to you our dear friend, Miss Mitford — no prude — no fanatic—yet one who said or implied to me once, that a woman should not be eager to praise Leigh Hunt—or something to that effect. Now *I*, you know, am proud to be eager to praise him—you know it as well as I.

" Still there *are* passages of his early works which strike both at morals and at religion—not in the person of anybody— not by a mistaken leniency (if any leniency can be mistaken) towards persons—nor at sectarianism or nice superfluities of dogma. Neither I nor you can deny these things; but the poet has done better by cancelling them in new editions. You know Shelley, in the midst of the grand signatures of God, wrote at Chamouni—ἄθεος. Poor Shelley!—he lied against himself, as against the Creator. For 'every true poet,' says a true poet (and one so happy, as a thinker, as never to change his opinions !) has a religious passion in his soul. *

"And I won't try to slay you with

* This hit was meant for me. I may here say that Leigh Hunt had a religious passion *in his soul.*

your sword. And I will believe readily
and gladly upon your testimony that
your friend—whom I should be proud to
have for my friend—is a religious man,
as he is a true poet. Of a devotional
nature he could not choose but partake.
I agree with you that the cordiality and
benignity of his genius are essentially
Christian. And may I say of myself
that I hope there is nobody in the world
with a stronger will and aspiration to
escape from *sectarianism* in any sort or
sense, when I have eyes to discern it,—
and that the sectarianism of the National
Churches, to which I do not belong, and
of the Dissenting bodies, to which I do—
stand together before me on a pretty just
level of detestation? Truth (as far as
each thinker can apprehend) apprehended
—and love, comprehending—make my
idea—my hope of a Church. But the

Christianity of the world is apt to wander from Christ and the hope of Him.

"Where *I* am wandering, you will wonder. I wonder a little myself. I should be thanking you instead, perhaps, for this new sight of new printer's proofs, and all the pleasure they have given me. I like very much indeed your estimate of Landor;—laughed—as well as such wights as I can laugh—at your genius of the drama with a cast-net, and at some other things—and clapped my hands mentally over sayings of more gravity. He, Landor, will be pleased, I think; and you have done your 'spiriting' excellently. Just as you tell me, I intrude my suggestions on the margin. I perceived on the other proof that you had not revised it, and I perceived in this, that you have done so but partially.

" I return the proof to-day, because I foresee that even if I detain it till to-morrow I shall not have time to write about Tennyson. So my words about him must follow instead of accompanying it.*

" It will be delightful to me to praise Tennyson — although, by St. Eloy, I never imitated him; and I take that oath, because Mr. —— thought I instructed my readers how to say ' ed ' at his suggestion, and because the *Quarterly* was of opinion that, if it hadn't been for him, I should have hung a lady's hair ' blackly ' instead of ' *very* blackly.' The ' very ' melting of the heaven of criticism —a rank plagiarism !—only the veri-ty of it is far from being plain to me, what-

* This refers to the article on Tennyson which was written by me, and sent in proof-sheets for Miss Barrett to interpolate.

ever may be the verisimilitude. But if the 'New Spirit of the Age' should say so too, by St. Eloy again, I will not reproach, reprove, or murmur. What a wandering, rollingstone I am to-day, to be sure! In good sooth, thinking over my letter of some days ago, and of the great tempest which appeared to me awaiting you in the form of the disappointed vanities of sundries,—it occurred to me that you would rationally infer the probability of my judging, in the matter, from my own proper consciousness of offensible self-love. Now I beg you not to infer so any more. I do not say, 'Tell the truth of me,' because of course you will tell it as you discern it. But I may promise you not to murmur, not to be angry, not to be vexed —('methinks the lady doth protest too much')—by any unpleasant truth which is necessary for you to say. So, *nota bene*—when I talked of 'thunder, lightning, and of rain,' it was not my thunder. You will have plenty, nevertheless.

"That will do for to-night, surely, in the way of mist. You shall have Tennyson [her interpolations] this week.

"Ever yours,

"E. B. B."

It is not only because the corporal presence of Miss Barrett, Leigh Hunt, and Miss Mitford has passed away that I consider myself at liberty to divulge a name mentioned to me, in the second paragraph of this letter, thirty years ago; but because what was said can no longer be any source of annoyance or unpleasantness to the relatives and friends of the party most concerned (Miss Mitford), and also because it was so sincerely

her opinion that I am sure she would feel
no objection to have it recorded.

I have described Miss Mitford as a
lady of the " old school; " and I may now
add that she had a horror of modern
French romances, and most of the fash-
ionable English novelists into the bar-
gain.   They were not to be compared to
Miss Ferrier, Miss Austen, Miss Edgeworth, and Mrs. Inchbald.   Nor *are* they
in many respects—always excepting some
of the great writers, such as George Sand
and Victor Hugo.   But Miss Mitford
shook her head even at those writers.
True, she was of large sympathies intellectually, and "no prude," but she
shrank from the mere mention of the
names of Fourrier and Robert Owen, and
in fact from every writer who seemed to be
undermining the existing condition of
society in its religious and moral oonven-

tionalities, its habits, customs, and manners. Moreover, she was a "country lady," and if she caught any author growing a snowdrop and crocus at the wrong time of the year, he never recovered a place in her memory. On a certain occasion she had been speaking of the rabbit-shooting at Bear Wood; and afterwards happening to propose a visit there, I inadvertently remarked that I should be very happy to accompany her, but that of late years I had taken to gymnastic exercises, and quite given up all field sports—besides, "I didn't care for rabbit shooting." It was the wrong season !—and the look and exclamation that followed, showed me that I had lost something of my position in her mind for ever. It says much for a local literary reputation "in the country" when a lady living in a cottage —a real cottage—almost covered with roses, jessamine, honeysuckle, and an apricot-tree spreading all over the south wall—who, giving an evening party, with no "spread" whatever, beyond tea and coffee and a prodigality of strawberries, shall yet have had a line of private carriages waiting outside, astonishing the little hedges of the highway and green lanes for nearly half a mile, and bringing the *élite* of the county families for miles all round. What could such a hostess feel and think of any writers who seemed to be "flying in the face" of all this elegance, respectability, and landed property, not to speak of clerical magnates, and the narrow white ties and cut-away waistcoats of accomplished curates from every little spire in the vicinity!

A most excellent person was Mary Russell Mitford, but she did not understand or know Leigh Hunt—and she certainly did not wish to do either. Her estimate of Dickens was not much more complimentary. She could not admire his love of "low life;" yet she did not perceive that a genuine country clodpole of Berkshire or elsewhere was about as low a type of man as could well be found, such as makes one think that Darwin's theory need by no means require millions —or even many thousands—of years.

XXX.   " Monday Morning.

[Date probably about 1848.]

"I answer your note before you can answer mine, and it is the best so. Whatever may be said or unsaid, of me and mine in your work [alluding to the forthcoming 'New Spirit of the Age'], do not give a second thought to any imagination of discontent as applicable to me. I shall know that you meant the kindest

—and understand *awry* everything not the pleasantest. My head will not go round.

"For the rest, or rather under the whole, if I myself am not *tame* about the 'Seraphim,' it is because I am the person interested. I wonder to myself sometimes, in a climax of dissatisfaction, how I came to publish it. It is a failure in my own eyes; and if it were not for the poems of less pretension in its company, would have fallen, both probably and deservedly, a dead weight from the press.

"Something I shall do hereafter in poetry, I hope. Hopes which have fallen dead from all things, are thrown in a heap *there* — perhaps like withered leaves! We must hope in something however, if we live.

"Which I did not mean to say in beginning this note.

" Only you will see that I shall not be discontented at the effects of your comments, etc. ; it is better too, perhaps, so. The book [the critical work in preparation] will be in better odour for it, with the million.

" Ever truly yours,

"E. B. B.

" I heard from Miss Mitford this morning. She appears resolved to go to Jersey, as you know probably."

" Saturday.

". My dear Mr. Horne,—I send you ' an opinion ' on Tennyson. Use it, or do not use it. He is a divine poet; but I have found it difficult (in the examination of my own thoughts of him) to analyse his divinity, and to determine (even to myself) his particular aspect as a writer. What is the reason of it ? It never struck me before. A true and divine poet nevertheless.

" Have you a portrait of him ? I hope so.

" Yours,

" E. B. B."

Miss Mitford considered that music should have been cultivated by me rather than poetry, except only so far as dramatic literature was concerned ; and she often threw out very pointed hints to that effect, as may be gathered from the opening of the following letter :—

XXXI.   " December 18th, 1848.

" Thank you, my dear Mr. Horne. Your note amused me extremely. And I am very glad, since you excite me to disinterested virtue by seeming to expect it, that you have a month's more ' leave ' for the book. It was certainly

most hard upon you to be pressed into
press by such thumbscrewing. But the
two volumes were resolved on long ago,
were they not ? Miss Mitford told me of
them a month since.

" As to music and poetry, I know perfectly well how it was—although I asked
you the question. ' Orion ' is something
more than playing on an instrument; it is
composition in the manner of Beethoven,
who was a poet if ever there was one.
What you say of comparisons has truth
in it. And yet do you not know that the
metaphysicians declare the impossibility
of discovering any object, or even straight
line, *without two colours ?* And the analogy is favourable to the use of comparisons; moreover, Plutarch and Mr.
Horne have had frequent recourse to
them.

" But there is another reason why

poetry should not be compared with the
other arts, *i.e.*, because poetry contains
them all. Is this not true? And then
for a poet to prefer being a musician
(even in the great composing sense) is an
inconsequence of reason as well as an
ingratitude of genius which I never seriously attributed to you, although somebody made affidavit to me that it was
so in fact; and that you didn't care
much about poetry after all—not you!
And you, the poet of 'Orion'! It was
monstrous on the face of it. Only if
people will play like Orpheus, other
people's ideas of them will be apt to
grow bewildered in the running under-
wood—entangled in the branches—lost
in the shadows. And I think I have
heard that you compose as well as play
on harp, lute, sackbut, dulcimer, and all
manner of instruments.

" Mr. Reade—his dagger !

" After all, I am not a ' good hater.'
Have not, I do assure you (and you may
think the worse of me for it, perhaps !), a
single personal animosity in the world ;
and also I am tolerably good tempered,—
that is, I never threw the chairs about
the room in a passion since I was eleven
years old. Therefore, altogether, it is
easy for me to comprehend that your
friend, albeit a foe of mine, is one of the
most amiable and cultivated men in the
world ; and to pardon him heartily for
my having displeased him. ' Liberté,
égalité, ou la mort ! ' We may each
think as we like of each other's poetry,
and no harm done to either. My objection, however, to certain volumes, is not
so much that they are Mr. Reade's, as
that *they are not his.*

" I am so glad that you have Tennyson's

portrait. Do you know that he is not at all in good health just now? I heard it the other day with great regret.

"Do you want 'an opinion' upon Monckton Milnes? or have you had enough of me? I admired his first volume very much; but his later poetry seems to want fire and imagination, and to strain too much at the didactic. His poetry for the people is poetry for the sages—deficient, it strikes me, in all popular qualities. And then that exquisite 'Lay of the Humble' which I was praising lately, and which affected me much at the time I read it (it appeared in the first volume), somebody told me the other day that it was not original. Taken from the German I think they said it was. I wish I knew. It is very beautiful in any case.

"*Blackwood* gave a paper—a review—

once, between Mr. Milnes and me, and I was very proud of the association.

" Faithfully your privy councillor,

" E. B. B."

XXXII. "Dec. 22nd, 1843.

" Just ten minutes before your note came, I held Monckton Milnes's volumes in my hands—the two first, at least— having bethought me of taking an opportunity of borrowing them from Mr. Kenyon. So now, if you please, I will make a few notes on them, which you will 'improve' (literally) to the edification of your readers afterwards. And in the meantime—I am very patient, you know, but in the meantime I should like to hear what you want me to do, and what this great subject to come is. I confess to being moderately curious about it. 'Not Dr. Pusey.' Thank you for

the '*not.*'   And not a political economist,
I hope—not a mathematician, nor a man
of science—such a one as Babbage, for
instance, to undo me.   My dear Mr.
Hcrne, certainly I am a little beset with
business just now, being on the verge of
getting another volume into print,—
with one or two long poems struggling
for completion at my hands, in order to
a subsequent falling upon the printer's.
But if there should be nothing likely to
take much time, in the work you medi-
tate for me, I shall be very happy, at
present and always, to be of use to you,
or trying to do it,—which, as I say it
honestly, I hope you will act as if you
believed.   Thank you much for the
promise of proofs, and you will tell me
what the new subject is?   Not that I
am impatient.   Oh, no!

"And so you heard of 'Tennyson and

Mr. Sterling.'   Well ! there is no accounting for tastes, as we say with proverbial
wisdom ; and, what is quite as certain,
there is no accounting for want of taste.
Mr. Sterling is admired by some, I am
aware, and I would rather that you had
your impressions of him from reading his
book, uncoloured by hearing what I say.
He was a contributor to *Blackwood ;* and
some two or three years ago, published
his contributed poems in an independent
form,—just as Mr. Simmons has done.
By the way, there are persons who think
highly of Mr. Simmons,—for instance,
Miss Mitford does, praising him for
terseness and vigour.   To return to Mr.
Sterling, I never read his book, although
I have read many of his poems in *Blackwood.*   He falls, to my appreciation, into
the class of respectable poets ; good
sense and good feeling, somewhat dry

and cold, and very level, smooth writing being what I discern in him. There are Mr. Sterling, Mr. Simmons, Lord Leigh, and one or two others, who have education and natural ability enough to be anything in the world, *except* poets, and who choose to be poets ' in spite of nature and their stars,' to say nothing of gods, men, and critical columns. Moreover, all these writers, by a curious consistency, take up and use the Gallic-Drydeny conception of versification,—so, at least, the passing glances I have had of their proceedings lead me to suppose. Now, you will judge for yourself, dear Mr. Horne, and I shall not be uneasy lest you should fall into prejudices in consequence of my hasty impressions."

XXXIII.   " Dec. 23rd, 1843.

" I forgot, after all. Agnes Strickland

is the author of the 'Mémoirs of the
Queens of England,' by which she is
principally known. She did, however,
write before—tales, I think—perhaps a
novel; but, although one of the very best
read persons of your acquaintance, in all
manner of romances and novels—good,
bad, and indifferent,—I do feel rather
in a mist about her doings in these
respects, only having a faint idea that
I have looked through a volume or two
of hers, and that I found them of the
highly moral, didactic, and useful-know-
ledge-society description. But do not
trust me an inch, for I feel in a mist,
and in a sort of fear of confounding the
maiden didactication of Mrs. Ellis when
she was Sarah Stickney, and this of Miss
Strickland's,—having been given to confound Stickneys and Stricklands from the
very beginning. One or two volumes of

the ' Memoirs of the Queens of England '
I have read ; and they seemed to me to
show industry and good taste in the
selection and compilation of materials.
But I did not read any more, just because
I like the old Chronicles, and dislike the
compiling spirit.   Miss Lawrence, you
are aware, has published Memoirs of
the Queens also,—and, moreover, the
two ladies have stood at cocked-pistol
in relation to one another, because
of this coincidence of subject.   I have
not seen Miss Lawrence's work, but,
from indications of extracts, I do more
than suspect that she is the deeper-
minded woman of the two, and qualified to take, in literature, the higher
place.

"By the way, either a Stickney or a
Strickland wrote ' The Poetry of Life,'—
prose (very) essays, which I couldn't get

to the end of—full of words, and signifying nothing.*

" I confess that I wondered a good deal at Mr. Buckingham's, or the Literary Institute's, selection of Miss Strickland as the second female Honorary Member. Nobody else to be found fit for the honour, except Miss Strickland!   And Miss Martineau, Mrs. Jameson, Maria Edgeworth, Mary Howitt, and Lady Morgan all alive —with long-established European reputations! France and Germany will be a little astonished, I think; and, for my own part, although it gave me cordial pleasure to hear of the honour won by, and honourably paid to, Miss Mitford, I should have been more pleased, even for her sake, and valued the appreciation more fully, if it had united her name to the names of these distinguished contem-

* See Section V., " Last Letters."

poraries, rather than severed it from them.

" Truly yours,
" E. B. B."

XXXIV.   " January 5th, 1844,
" Friday Night and Saturday Morning.

" My majesty was astounded at the impromptu of a chapter on the novelists, sent by electricity to Windsor. A pile of ' commands ' took fire, and was consumed on the spot. It is a very clever paper. Tell me who wrote it—in a very small whisper. You tell me always to write on the margin, and I suppose I take for granted that you wish it, and have other proofs for use. Otherwise I should never, I think, go on blotting so impudently the length and breadth of my opiniativeness.

" And, my dear Mr. Horne, it really

does strike me strongly that you and
your critic do no manner of justice to
Mrs. Trollope, who is a very clever writer
—very acute—absolute over laughter in
matters of caricature on the coarse scale,
and moreover—which scarcely accords
with her general character as either you
or I consider it—a vivid and graphic
painter of scenic nature. Because I said
this illegibly somewhere in the proof I
say it over again here. I am determined
that you shall read me. Also Mrs. Gore's
wit should be specially mentioned. She
is ' almost feminine,' tell your critic, in
the flashing of her wit. Also, Mr. James
is praised far too much, to my mind.
Also, such a writer as Banim, a true
genius, should have been mentioned in
the body of your article. You might
have done it in a paragraph. Also, there
is another omission which I shall never

end talking of, if it prove to be actually
an omission. Do you mean calmly,
advisedly, and with your eyes open, to
have a chapter on the novelists and omit
Bulwer? Or do you (which would be a
satisfactory explanation) give him a room
to himself? But if so, why not refer to
him in this paper as a leader in the highest
class of the art, to be mentioned hereafter? Think of 'Ernest Maltravers,'
and 'Alice,' worth all the historical novels
—I was near saying that ever were
written! You, a poet and dramatist, to
forget the passionate unity of that great
work! for the two romances complete the
single work. And then, even if you suc-
ceed in lifting the historical romance over
the head of all other kinds of romance
(a position which I protest solemnly and
vociferously against—as untenable and
unworthy of a poet's editorship), by that

very sign, Sir Lytton Bulwer takes throne rank in his ' Pompeii' and ' Rienzi,' while Mr. James lies under the footstool. Not that I would dishonour Mr. James. He is a picturesque writer, and paints his canvas-deep figures in bright costume, and in the midst of excellent landscape. Often when I have been very unwell, I have been able to read his books with advantage, when I could not read better ones. You may read him from end to end without a superfluous beat of the heart,—and they are just the sort of intellectual diet fitted for persons ' ordered to be kept quiet ' by their physicians. Do not mistake, I am writing quite gravely, and not, I hope, ungratefully. I am grateful to Mr. James for many a still serene hour. I have every respect for him as a sensible level writer—a very agreeable writer—pure-minded, and with talents in his own province. But to give him place as a romance writer over Bulwer, the prose poet of the day, and over Banim, the prose-dramatist, is, must be, a monstrous exaggeration of his actual claim. Besides, this measuring of novelists' merits by their ' regular issue ' strikes me as a false step in itself. Such is my protestation.

" Tell me, did you ever read ' Ernest Maltravers,' with its sequence of ' Alice ' ? I suspect *nay*, or you would not in your editorship be so patient. It appears to me that you cultivate scorn for the novel-readers, or else have no comprehension for them, dividing them into classes of Godwin - readers, Fielding - readers, Richardson-readers, James-readers, and so forth. You have no sympathy for persons who, when they were children, beset everybody in the house, from the proprietor to the second housemaid, to 'tell them a story;' and retain so much of their childhood—green as grass—as that love of stories. If a reader reads Smollett for the literature, I can quite comprehend how the same reader could not read Richardson, and *a fortiori* how James would be an insipid sort of *caviare* to him. But when the taste for fiction is a thing distinct from the taste for literature, the very same persons may seize upon the story of a hundred story-tellers, and love, for the sake of it, the 'makings' of even inferior hands. Oh, that love for story-telling! It may be foolish, to be sure; it leads one into waste of time and strong excitements, to be sure; still, how pleasant it is! How full of enchantment and dream-time gladnesses! What a pleasant accompaniment to one's lonely coffee-cup in

the morning or evening, to hold a little
volume in the left hand and read softly
along how Lindoro saw Monimia over
the hedge, and what he said to her!
After breakfast we have other matters
to do—grave 'business-matters,' poems
to write upon Eden, or essays on Carlyle, or literature in various shapes to
be employed seriously on.   But everybody must attend to a certain proportion of practical affairs of life, and
Lindoro and Monimia bring us ours.
And then, if Monimia behaves pretty
well, what rational satisfaction we have
in settling her at the end of the book.
No woman who speculates and practises
'on her own account' has half the
satisfaction in securing an establishment
that we have with our Monimias, nor
should have, let it be said boldly.   Did
we not divine it would end so—albeit

ourselves and Monimia were weeping
together at the end of the second
volume? Even to the middle of the
third, when Lindoro was sworn at for
a traitor by everybody in the book,
may it not be testified gloriously of *us*
that *we* saw through him, and relied
implicitly upon an exculpating fidelity
which should be ' in ' at the finis, to
glorify him finally? What, have you
known nothing, Mr. Editor, of these
exaltations? Indeed your note looks
like it. I could almost fancy you
hadn't, by this talk of ' taste, taste,'
and of readers turned to St. Leon who
never could read anything else. The
love of fiction, as such, escapes you
wholly. I could almost fancy that you
never felt inclined even to commit jus-
tifiable homicide on an individual who,
having read the book you are reading,

and beholding you with tears in your eyes over the thickest of the sorrows of it, should venture to inform you that Monimia will get over it all in the second volume. But indeed this is scarcely credible. Here I am writing as if neither you nor I had anything to do in the 'varsal world.' Forgive me, or try.

"And mind you don't show the proof with my pertnesses on it to your critic. Trusting to you, I never care for what I write, but let it go to you as it comes to me.

"Ever truly yours,
"E. B. B."

There must have been some misinformation or misunderstanding with regard to the accusation of a breach of confidence made in the following letter :—

XXXV.   "January 8th, 1844.

"MY DEAR MR. HORNE,—I begin to
believe in the force of my own incanta-
tions, which is certainly half-way to
witchhood. Yes, the writer's analysis is
warm with feeling and sympathy—and
I am very glad of it. Is it not true that
such romances as Bulwer's are of a far
higher class than the historical novel?
I think so—I am sure of it.

"When I took breath after my long
letter the other day, I began to remember (too late), that not a word had
been said, on either side, of Dickens.
Only your remembering and esteeming
Dickens was sure,—and I had it in my
head, by some occult means, that you
were inclined to forget Bulwer on purpose.
I have known depreciators of Bulwer—a
friend of ours being one. He is called
" false " and " unhealthy " by a certain

school of critics and readers, in whose eyes all intensity wears the aspect of extravagance.

" And now, without being extravagant, I am about to be intensely angry with you—and to illustrate my own critical views. This morning I received a letter from Mr. Merry, of Stonefield, with whom I do not regularly correspond, but who insisted, against my will, on my writing about his book on 'predestination,' and when I did so, branched off himself into a collateral commentary on the English liturgy, in relation to certain supposed views of mine. I send you a leaf of his letter, the body of which refers to theological matters; and you may thus judge, by your own eyes and judgment, how surprised I was to read what he says of Mr. Reade—you may judge yourself what the evidence is of

Mr. Horne's high treason. You are the *only person* to whom I ever spoke or hinted one word in reference to the supposed opinion of me. If I wrote as I did to you—it was wrong of me, perhaps —but it was written in absolute confidence, and with the faith that you wouldn't expose all my nonsense to the third person immediately concerned. Perhaps after all this was expecting more of you than I had had sense enough to do for myself,—but you will be just enough to testify that I never *complained* (as I had no reason) of any opinion attributed, by conjecture or otherwise, to Mr. Reade or others, on the subject of my writings. There is plenty of fault in them, as nobody knows better than myself; and even if there were no fault, I should be the last in the world to complain of a free opinion in its full expression, because I was the object of its condemnation. If I mentioned it at all to you, it was incidentally —and *I never have* mentioned it to another—*never*, not even to Miss Mitford. And as to Mr. Merry, Mr. Reade's name never before has occurred between us two.

"Et tu Brute!—oh—to go and betray me before the ides of March!

"It was written, you see, that we should quarrel a little about Mr. Reade —who certainly 'knows more than he should do' by questionable means— albeit not a witch. Perhaps you made a portable packet of some of my letters, and sent them to amuse his leisure withal, or 'read them into the air,' with intention! Which would account for the 'caustic touches' by return of post.

"I shall write to Mr. Merry, and beg him to assure Mr. Reade that I never considered myself in the slightest degree aggrieved by any opinion of his, of whatever nature I might have supposed that opinion to be. I shall treat the subject in a general way and without mentioning *you*. That Mr. Reade is worthy of every respect, and too amiable a man to give pain, or think or speak harshness of any individual, I have always believed and continue to believe of him, and shall add the expression of that belief to the rest.

"'Something too much of this.' I hope I may have appeared in a sufficient passion in the course of my letter.

" Truly yours,
" E. B. B."

What the presentation volume was

that the next letter acknowledges, I
have not the remotest recollection, nor
do I remember what occasioned the gift,
unless, indeed, as Miss Barrett had ren-
dered me so much literary assistance,
and I could not venture to offer her any
recompense of the ordinary kind, it may
have been that something was substituted
which I thought she would have no objection to accept.

XXXVI.   "Monday.
                    [Postmark—Jan. 80th, 1844.]

"I could almost quarrel with you, and
be sure of being right withal, in defiance
of prophecy (if I had the heart), for
sending me this far too expensive
present. How could you do so, my
dear Mr. Horne? It is a splendid book.
What visions of beauty! There is a
spirit in the leaves. But the spirit

of the kindness is the over-mastering
one.

"I think, from a far remembrance,
that Mrs. Norton's first poem was called
'The Undying One.' Her chief poem,
that is, the principal one in her last
volume, is 'The Dream.' Have you read
these, to be of opinion still, as said the
Quarterly, that she is a modification of
Byron? The only poems which could
have suggested such a likeness are the
personal ones, I fancy; and they, with
some intensity and much pathos, are
very unlike Byron, I must hold. 'Less
vindictive!'—ah, Mr. Horne, do *you* too
call Byron vindictive? *I* do not. If
he turned upon the dart, it was by the
instinct of passion, not by the theory of
vengeance, I believe and am assured.
Poor, poor Lord Byron! Now would I
lay the sun and moon against a tennis-

ball that he had more tenderness in one section of his heart than * * * * has in all hers, though a tenderness misunderstood and crushed, ignorantly, profanely, and vilely, by false friends and a pattern wife. His blood is on our heads—on us in England—even as [the First] Napoleon's is! Two stains of the sort have we in one century; and what will wash them out?

" There is a poem, much shorter than the first, and yet longer than the mere lyrics (in ' The Dream, and other Poems'), the title of which I forget, with a domestic subject, and written in stanzas, which has, to my apprehension, more power than any other composition of Mrs. Norton's. Some of her songs for music are very lovely; and her lyrics of more *body* have the qualities of sweetness and pathos to a touching and thrilling degree.

'The Dream' you may like better than I do. The personal references in the miscellaneous poems go deep and true, and are as tenderly written as ink mixed with tears can write anything. My wager of the sun and moon intended no depreciation of this tenderness.

" Find out the domestic poem, which is not, by the way, a personal poem. It will strike you, I think; and our critics may say that it is ' almost masculine ' in characteristic power. You should re-member, moreover, that she composes music, published with her own words. Also, did she not edit at one time either the *Court Journal* or the *Belle Assem-blée*? And she has contributed prose tales full of colour and expression to various annuals.

" My earnest request to you is *not* to take for granted anything I say; but to look into the poems yourself. Mary Howitt's ballads are nearer and dearer to *me*, and suggestive of a far higher species of poetical power, according to my view, than any volume I ever saw of Mrs. Norton's: and then you know how prejudices work, and I confess to you a little disinclination . . . which may vibrate, in spite of me, through my estimate of Mrs. Norton's writings. Now, mind, I do not say *it is so*, but that it *may be so;* and I put you on your guard *lest* it be so. She has the face of an angel, and the tongue of a wit; but tender and pitiful to woman, as a woman should be, she is not; and for this I cannot easily pardon her. I do not speak out of personal experience.

"With thanks once again, believe me,

"Truly yours,

"E. B. B."

I did not fail to communicate to Miss Barrett that I accepted her admission as to "how prejudices work," and with especial reference to the injured lady in question. As usual, there was a post-script, with something good in it.

"*I* should have forgotten Mrs. S. C. Hall, too, only just as I was writing to you, came a note from her to me with some proposition about a new magazine —a lady's magazine! So I bethought me of naming her to you—and you *must* make room for her."

Our next letter refers to two celebrities of that day who deserve to be equally celebrated now, though I fear that is not the case.

XXXVII. "Wednesday—[1844] Thursday, rather. [Written after midnight, I suppose.]

"MY DEAR. MR. HORNE,—The poem which I called ' domestic ' is one, I think,

in an octave stanza containing a story
—the history of a wife who becomes
aware of the dishonour of her husband.
It succeeds 'The Dream.' It has more
power than any composition of Mrs.
Norton's which I have read. The name
quite escapes me ; and I have so painful
an association of a personal nature with
the book, as to lose all courage to look
into it. There are domestic poems also,
which refer to herself personally—and to
the pictures of her children—sweet and
tender.

"In respect to Barry Cornwall, I am
delighted to hear that you admit him ;
and the first omission was probably
accidental, or from reasons of time and
haste. His lyrical poems are most exquisite,—like an embodied music. In
the melodies of words he is learned, and
in the causes of tears not uninstructed.

His dramatic fragments are not masculine;
—but *Ford* was not masculine—when he
wrote alone. They seem to me to have
dramatic intonations, moving, if not
deep. His fault is only felt in a con-
tinuous reading, when we become aware
of a certain sameness—a one-tonedness,
which is not the tone of a trumpet. It
is a more effeminate instrument. In my
own private opinion, Barry Cornwall has
done a good deal, with all his genius,
and, perhaps as a consequence of his
genius, to emasculate the poetry of the
passing age. To talk of 'fair things'
when he had to speak of women, and
of 'laughing flowers' when his business
was with a full-blown daisy [dame, or
dairymaid] is the fashion of his school.
His care has not been to use the most
expressive, but the prettiest word. His
Muse has held her Pandemonium too

much in the cavity of his ear. Still, that this arises from a too exquisite sense of beauty as a *means* as well as an object, is evident; and for all sweet and exquisitely pathetic lyric qualities, we need not go farther than to Barry Cornwall.

" In this last republication, I miss (it may be there, but running the book through hastily, I cannot find it) what used to thrill me through and through with the charm of lyric cadence and matchless pathos. I admired it so, that I used the stanza in that slight poem of my own, called ' Loved once,'—only *reversing* it in every second verse. But the time ran in my head :—

'Must it be ?   Then, farewell !
Thou, whom my woman's heart has loved too long,
    Farewell—and be this song,
The last in which I say, I loved thee well.'

It begins so, I remember, and the whole

lyric is most moving. I wish I had it to send you.

" You know his ' Marcian Colonna,' and others perhaps which I do not know. I admire Barry Cornwall much.

" Mr. Moxon was good enough to send me yesterday Mr. Patmore's poems. I had not time to cut the leaves, when Miss Mitford came, and I gave her the first-fruits of the book. Between you and me — ' dreadfully private ' — this would have been more generous of me, if I had not by a few glances nearly satisfied myself that he is *not* a Tennyson, and never could have been. Also, he is not to be reproached with Barry Cornwall's fault of over-effluence in music. Still, I have no right to judge—for the leaves are uncut.

" I heard of your meeting Mr. Chorley in Miss Mitford's presence. It never struck her what a meeting of thunder-clouds it might be—until I made the suggestion.

"I shall do my book the honour of placing your name in it, and prove that we are not under different banners,—and that .

"I am,

"Ever faithfully and gratefully yours,

"E. B. B.

"I must thank you (having forgotten it before) for your criticism about 'the many miles.' Certainly I made out by the loose expression that Eve had travelled many miles in one day—which might have been? though I wish I had the power of altering it."

I do not think Miss Barrett does adequate justice to Barry Cornwall (Mr.

Procter) as a *dramatist*. His tragedy of "Mirandola" (finely produced by Macready, who personated the principal part) is one among various marked instances that must occur to all who are conversant with the dramatic literature of the last five-and-thirty years, — that the "decline," as its disgusting *fall* before "burlesque" is softly termed, is certainly not attributable to the want of dramatists of genius. Of the foregoing critique by Miss Barrett, no portion was inserted in the "New Spirit of the Age," as the intended paper was crowded out, but reserved for a projected third volume, which, however, never was written. The remark on a possible "meeting of thunder-clouds," alludes to a somewhat painful, and at any rate an awkward and ridiculous scene. The late Mr. Henry Chorley, an accomplished gentleman, of fine and delicate tastes, was writing critiques in the *Athenæun*, and elsewhere, during the time that the Syncretic Society (mainly composed of un-acted dramatists and dramatic performers) was in " full flourish ; " and he often attacked them, and was found of employing the epithet of " feeble." Extravagant they often no doubt were, and boastful, and now and then absurd in their sanguine views of rapidly reviving the British Drama, even to the Elizabethan height; but they meant well, their cause was good, they were full of energy and faith, and for the most part were certainly not " feeble." It chanced at this time that I had written a sort of Christmas book for children, called " The London Doll," and in one of the chapters somebody says,—I forget who, perhaps the " Doll," —" It was a moment of that

terrible kind, as the poet Henry Chorley
says,—.

‘ When all that's feeble squeaks within the soul ! ’ ”

A copy of this little book had been
sent by me to Mary Howitt. Mr. Henry
Chorley chanced to call upon her a morning or so afterwards, and Mary Howitt,
with the innocence of a child of seven
years old, placed the book in his hand,
as she was leaving the room to attend
to some domestic matter, calling his attention to the (assumed) quotation from
“ the poet, Henry Chorley,” as something complimentary that would please
him. When she returned, “ the poet ”
was staring down at the open book !
“ Why,” said he, “ look here, Mrs.
Howitt ! ”—but the scene is too ridiculous
to pursue. With regard to the “ number
of miles ” that Miss Barrett made Eve
journey during a single night, I had

written to ask if she intended Eve to
have had wings, or to have been assisted
by winged spirits, because Eve as a
human being could not have got over
the distance indicated, in the exhausted
state of her feelings. But the poem
being printed, I tried to soften the vexation by directing the attention of the
poetess to a similar oversight made by
Chaucer, not as to distance, but the pro-
gress of time. In the "Knighte's Tale,"
we find Palamon and Arcite taken prisoners—say, at about the age of twenty-
five. They are shut up in a tower, and
"thus passeth year by year,"—say, four
or five years; and then they both catch
sight of Emelie. After this we hear of
several events, each occupying "a year
or two." Then we are told that Palamon
has suffered "love and distress," during
seven years since he set eyes on Emelie.

Meanwhile Emelie also speaks of "full many a year." After the death of Arcite, we hear of "by processe and by length of certain years"—say, three or four more. I think it will be found that fourteen or fifteen years must have elapsed since the two young knights were taken prisoners; so that when Palamon marries Emelie, she cannot be less than thirty-five, nor he less than forty. This continuity may be admired, for its earnestness and intensity of purpose; but I much doubt if Chaucer directly intended so many years to elapse.

The article upon Charles Dickens was written entirely by myself, and Miss Barrett had never seen any portion of it until the work was published. The following letter contains some comments of a kind which I think no one else has ever made—that is, as matter of public criticism.

XXXVIII.   "Tuesday, February 20, 1844.

"I quite forgot to say to you, my dear Mr. Horne, what I think is your only omission of importance in your admirable critical essay upon Charles Dickens. It is the influence upon his mind, most manifest and undeniable, of the French school of imaginative literature. When people talk of Fielding and Smollett as being ideals and models before him, elected by his own judgment,—they (and even *you*) omit what consciously or unconsciously, 'in the body or out of the body, I cannot say,' Victor Hugo has been to him. Did you ever read the powerful, the wonderfully powerful 'Trois Jours d'un Condamné'—and will you (if you have read it) confront your recol-

lections of it with most of the tragic
saliences of ' Oliver Twist '—the scenes
about the Jew Fagin, his trial scene
and otherwise? Since, two or three
years ago, I went regularly through all
the romances of the gifted Frenchman,
my admiration for our countryman has
paled down paler and paler. The fact
is, that we have no such romance-writer
as Victor Hugo,—let us be as anti-Gallic
as we please. And anti-Gallicism is the
merest affectation at this hour of the
day, upon which all the burning-glasses
of French genius appear to be concentrated. The indelicacy and want of
elemental morality make another side
of the question : but the *genius* is just
as undeniable to me, as the sun would
be in Italy. George Sand, for instance,
is the greatest female genius the world
ever saw— [at this period, George Eliot

had not appeared] — at least, since
Sappho, who broke off a fragment of her
soul to be guessed by—as creation did
by its fossils. And George Sand, it is
remarkable, precisely like her prototype,
has suffered her senses to leaven her
soul—to permeate it through and through,
and make a sensual soul of it. She is
a wonderful woman, and, I hope, rising
into a purer atmosphere by the very
strength of her wing. And then, Balzac
—Eugene Sue—even the Soulies, and
the grade lower—we cannot *wish* them
to be popular in England, for obvious
reasons, but it is melancholy to look
round and see no such bloom of intellectual glory on our own literature, in
shutting our doors against theirs.

"I send you a letter, received this
morning from America, because there
is as much about you in it as about me.

"A Mr. W——, a New York book-
seller, brought a letter of introduction
to me some ten days ago,—and when I
was forced to decline seeing him, wrote
to introduce himself to me 'paternally,'
as being the first bearer of my poetry
into the new world. It was this gentleman who begged me to send him some
account of my 'cousin Mr. Tennyson;'
—Leigh Hunt having intimated somewhere that he was my cousin. [He
said this figuratively.] So as *you* give
me grand-paternal advice sometimes, see
what a number of distinguished relations
I have—inclusive of the New York book-
seller!

"I send you this letter of Mr. Mathews', a little for him as well as for
you; and would entreat you—you who
have the power—to use any just influence
within your power, in order to procure

him the critical courtesy he looks for among us. I have explained once to him, but I fear he does not understand, how *I* can do nothing at all—and that if I were to presume a step, upon the circumstance of my accidental connection with the *Athenæum*, Mr. Dilke would very properly laugh me to scorn for my pains. In the case of my own book, I shall let it float down the stream as other books. I never did otherwise, and never shall. You know, the very act of offering a civility to some editors is considered in the light of offering a bribe to a judge—and, in fact, it should *not* be done, as well as could not be done. Still, I am embarrassed, because I see plainly that Mr. Mathews thinks I can do something—the 'something' being out of my power. The *Athenæum* reviewed his poem 'On Man' the other day, and in admitting the ability, dwelt in a way likely to be offensive on the want of ' grace '—and I was very sorry, quite impotently. Well, if you have it in your power to help his works, and can do so honestly,—or if any friend of yours within your influence can do so honestly, you will, I am sure, remember Mr. Mathews. He has no ordinary degree of mental power, which is developing itself into light in America; and he is no imitator of English models—which is remarkable. Moreover, I believe him to be full of genial kindness and generosity, upright and warm-hearted, and so, for the best reasons, well worth serving.

" You have no time to hear me talk, and I have little time to talk in,—and therefore logically I am talkative this morning.

"Ever and truly yours,

"E. B. B.

"What I say of French literature *versus* our own of the day, refers of course to a particular department of it. The French have no rhythmetic poetry, from a defect in the language: and their poetry finds issue in prose, while ours (thank God, and blessings on our 'pure well of English undefiled') flows in its right channel. We have no business to complain, therefore, that we have not a chorus of prose poets, such as the French boast of at this moment."

Victor Hugo's "Trois Jours d'un Condamné" I had read, and regarded as the most perfect thing of the kind ever put to paper. As with the writer, so with the reader—we are intensely and minutely identified with all the inmost anguish of thought and sensation, in every stage of the process through those harrowing three days and nights. And yet the treatment of that trial-scene of Fagin must be considered strikingly original, full of touches of genius ; and the same must be said of several other tragic scenes in " Oliver Twist." That the natural bent of the genius of Charles Dickens was to what actors term *eccentric comedy*, and to broad farce, and richly humorous and often ridiculous caricatures, no doubt can exist; nevertheless, his tragic scenes, in low life, and indeed the very lowest, are obviously his own, and founded upon an absolute knowledge of those classes he describes with so much perfection. That he had received some influences from the works of Victor Hugo is likely and natural enough; and I discovered in one of his books a yet more direct influence from one of the very earliest, if not the earliest (as well as the almost forgotten), novelists of America, viz., Brockden Brown—a writer of very peculiar genius and originality.

The next letter alludes to my critique on the poetry of Miss Barrett. I only said there precisely what I thought and felt about it, and have never entertained or given expression to any other opinion. The poetess believed in my sincerity; nevertheless it was a nice and delicate matter for her to write about, which however she gets through with the ease of any truthful person who believes in the truthfulness of another.

XXXIX.   "March 5, 1844.

"MY DEAR MR. HORNE,—It has been haunting me all this morning, that you may be drawing the very last inference I should wish you to draw from my silence. But I have been so unwell that I could not even read; and the writing has been impossible; and people cry out even now, ' Why, surely you are not going to write ! '

"I *must* write. It is on my mind— and must be off it.

" First to thank you for the books, which it was such unnecessary kindness for you to send,—and then, for the abundant kindness in another way which will, at the earliest thought, occur to you. My only objection to the paper is, that the personal kindness is too evident. My objection, you will see, leaves me full of gratitude to you; and fills to the brim that Venetian goblet of former obligations, which never held any poison.

" You are guilty of certain exaggerations, however, in speaking of me, against which I shall oppose my *dele* as you allow me. For instance, I have not been 'shut up in one room for six or seven years,'—four or five would be nearer; and then, except on one occasion, I have not been for 'several weeks together in the dark' during the course of them. And then there is not a single 'elegant Latin verse' extant from my hand. I never cultivated Latin verses. And then (last and greatest) Miss Martineau's beautiful book ('Life in the Sick Room') was _not_ dedicated to _me_, whatever may be said or thought of it. I know that a current report attributed the honour to me; but there was no whisper of truth in the report, and you must contradict it in the new edition.*

* I feel consoled for these errors by the fact that they show very clearly that no MS. or proof of the article about herself had been forwarded to her,—a " critical " courtesy not so common among literary friends as may be supposed.

" There is nothing to alter—that is,
nothing to add—in relation to myself;
but there are some inaccuracies, as I
have explained to you, and not the least
is in your opening allusion to the
Quarterly Review article. Why you
should give that blow to poor Lady
E——, I really cannot conceive. She
writes nonsense often, taking it for in-
spiration,—and her words carry away
her thoughts, instead of *vice versa ;* but
the truth is that she has more imagination, more fire, more notion of what
poetry *is*, than half the ' ladies' graciously
affected by you. To raise Miss Lowe,
for instance (who is an accomplished
woman, and full of acquirement, I believe, but who certainly never wrote a
line of poetry in her life), over the head
of Lady E——, who has a faculty—who
has imagination, only is in fault through

letting it run to seed—is a very undeniable injustice to which I must call your
attention. Also, Caroline Southey should
have been mentioned with some distinction. She is a womanly Cowper,
with much of his sweetness, and some of
his strength, and there is much in her
poems to which the heart of the reader
leans back in remembrance. The real
ffence, done by that article in the *Quarterly*, was the *classification*. As far as I
am concerned at least, that was what I
disliked. And probably Mrs. Norton and
Caroline Southey felt it still more dis-
honouring. Mrs. Brooke, the *Maria del
Occidente*, has a faculty ;—but for all the
rest, Lady E——, the sacrificed 'lady of
rank,' is well worth them all put together,—and *that* is not praise.

"But it is only astonishing that, in a
work of this nature, you should not have

made more slips, I am sure, than you have. How beautifully it is adorned— 'got up.' Guess which head I prefer? Southwood Smith's. The power, the serenity, and sweetness of the whole expression, have exceedingly impressed me. Is Tennyson's like? It is an intellectual head, but the eyes seem blanker than his should be, and the lips want delicacy.* Dickens has the dust and mud of humanity about him, notwithstanding those eagle eyes.

"And I have been *so* amused this morning, by the sight of a letter from your friend Mr. R——, which Miss Mitford sent me. He has seen, forsooth, your advertisement, with no name of his in it!—but he is too sure of his position with posterity to care for *that* now,—

* This portrait, from the painting by Samuel Laurence, was the first ever published of Tennyson. —ED.

though once it would have saddened
him. He is quite aware now that all
the notices are written by personal
friends of the parties! You have indeed got one true poet, he sees—'in
spite of his little *isms*'—(whom in the
world can he mean?—has Wordsworth
any little *isms?*) Yes, and another—
the 'porcelain poet,' Tennyson, who,
however, 'will never do anything great
and spirit - stirring,' like Mr. R——'s
'I——*' and the rest—which is a comfort. But that Leigh Hunt should ever
be raised up to such a height, and that
the author of 'I——*' should 'live to
see it,' is quite astounding to him—
only he is rather glad than otherwise
of it, from motives of humanity—'It
may benefit him.' That Dickens, moreover, should be so 'elevated,' is another
marvel—*he*, who is to pass away, with

all his 'coarse caricatures,' in the period
of a lifetime. Altogether, Mr. R—— feels
precisely on the subject of this book 'as
Molière did' when he observed dis-
dainfully the successes of his contemporaries, who were to be forgotten in
twenty years. It is a sublime position.

"I cannot resist telling you this—
although you must lay it by directly
among our secrets—because, you see,
Miss Mitford sent me the letter, and
might think that I oughtn't to say a
word about it. But I cannot resist the
pleasure of communicating it to you.
See what a 'pure aspiration' is! How
pure—*how* noble! How free from 'envy,
malice, and all uncharitableness'! I
wouldn't have such an inward fretting
of the heart-strings for a good deal more
than the author of 'I——*'s' chances of
posterity.

"Nothing is said of *me*, of course. And this is disdain, not toleration.

"And now I come to tell you, that, thanking you twenty times for the promise of your aye or nay, on the MS. question—I have reasonably determined *not* to trouble you with it. When I asked I did not think of second editions. Nay, perhaps I did not think enough of anything. It was a request worthy, I doubt not, of the goddess of Unreason—and I recall it—but thankfully, believe me.

"Yours with many sorts of gratitude,

"E. B. B.

"I have written myself *up* again with this letter. It does me good to write to you, you see, and there is not much essentially the matter,—I shall probably be quite right again to-morrow."

The reference to Robert Montgomery

in the following letter should be explained. Soon after the "New Spirit of
the Age" had appeared, in which was a
trenchant critique on Montgomery for
which I alone was responsible,—an amusing but what might have been a most
unpleasant *contretemps* occurred. Having
accepted an invitation to dine with a
friend, I arrived at his house early, and
was shown into a room where a gentleman was sitting. With the door in his
hand, my host said loudly, "Mr. Horne,
Mr. Robert Montgomery;" and adding a
remark of a mischievous and cruelly em-
barrassing character, slammed the door,
leaving us alone! Then, and through
the whole course of the evening, Montgomery behaved so genially that we were
both of us entirely at our ease. It should
be remembered that in those days a man
was called out for much less.

XL.   " June 9, 1844,

" Friday night, ten o'clock.

" Thank you, my dear friend, for your note, which has set me at ease.   We are agreed, I hope, absolutely.   It is ' better not to do too much to the article,' and it is still better not to do anything.

" I write to-night with the especial desire of telling you that I think it not only possible, but probable, that you may dilate to your apprehension, with too extreme a sensitiveness, the depreciations of the world.   It is an odd sort of world — not over kind and generous and grateful, and we need not expect too much from it.   Still, we may take over-depressing views of it sometimes. For instance, you fancy that Mr. Serjeant Talfourd takes upon himself to be discontented with what you say of him. *I know to the contrary*. He was heard to say

a very few days ago—speaking of poets
or dramatists, I scarcely am sure of the
definite subject—' There is Horne, who is
worth twenty of them! A true man of
genius *he* is! But he has written a book
called the "New Spirit of the Age," which
is likely, I fear, to do him a great deal
of harm. I am quite satisfied with what
he says of me in it—indeed he has said
more than I had any reason to expect.
But with other people it is different, and
I hear a great many complaints.'

" Those were the very words (as far as
I can recollect the words repeated to me,
and so far as my informant was correct)
used by Mr. Talfourd. He seemed to be
perfectly satisfied personally, and if he
was not, I must say he was an unreason-
able man.

" As to Dickens, I have nothing to
observe, except my own wonder. Only,

as you have mistaken Talfourd's words, you may have mistaken his besides. 'A great many complaints' there will of course be. You have not always wadded your bludgeon, and you meant to give occasion for 'a great many complaints' in particular cases! And now we must admit that you have *not* quite crowned Bulwer up to his right. Bulwer is a man of genius, and your praise is cold. If I were Bulwer, I should *not* be satisfied; and as I am *not* Bulwer, I may say so.

"I am almost sorry at what you tell me about Robert Montgomery—sorry, in my sympathy for you. It is abashing to find a man morally noble whom, for whatever excellent reasons, we have been decrying intellectually. But *is* he morally noble? In the preface to his 'Luther,' in which he replies generally to the remarks of the critical press, the tone is

of the ignoblest and worst. Audacious
without dignity, violent without power,
virulent without the strength of a sar-
casm. Still, he may be better out of
print. If I were you I should certainly,
for the convenience of my own feelings,
avoid the intercourse. For the rest, I
wish that article out of the book. I
certainly do. I venture to fancy that it
is (comparatively, and on the whole) a
weak point, and better away from the
point of sight.

"What do you mean by ' complaints '
being ' hitherto on the safe side of friendship ' ? I do not understand. You do
not mean that anything which anybody
could choose to say of your paper on me,
that any possible and imaginable imaginary comment on it could affect the
friendship which subsists between us?
Why, if the paper itself had been as

unkind as it is kind and cordial—even in such a case—my part of the said friendship could hardly have been affected, except by the natural pain. How kind you have been to me for years! Do I not remember it? Could I forget it? Try to keep up your spirits about the book. I really think (as I have told you already) that you fancy more harm than exists. Miss Mitford comes to town on Monday for a week—not to this house.

> " Most truly yours,
> " E. B. B."

Several persons of eminence, and a good many who held popular positions of merit, were omitted from the two volumes of the " New Spirit of the Age " for want of space, but with a settled intention of including them in a third volume. Circumstances caused this intended publication to be too long postponed, and it was finally abandoned. But in the meantime Miss Barrett, being full to overflowing of all the knowledge required, sent me various letters, of which good use was made, but only in the way of hints for summary remarks.

Here is one of them :—

XLI.   "Monday Morning.
[Postmark—Sept. 6th, 1844.]

" MY DEAR MR. HORNE—I am taking fright about the proofs, and begin to think it would be wiser to have no more of them, particularly as you are going out of town. I am secret as the first cousin of Harpocrates himself; but I was born without the faculty of what is called 'presence of mind,'—and an accident might betray us. Therefore no

proofs, while you are out of town, unless
I can do any good in correcting. *

"Certainly you must speak of Mrs.
S. C. Hall, and you may do so kindly and
justly at once. She has written one or
two novels; but the performances she is
better known by are her miscellaneous
light essays and tales, with which the
periodical literature of the day is sown
abundantly, and characteristic sketches
illustrative of her native Ireland, of
which she published a volume not long
ago, in conjunction with her husband.
Mr. S. C. Hall edits books of gems and
ballads, etc., up to monthly magazines.
His wife was an intimate friend of poor

---

* The nervous apprehensions of any lady in delicate health, who is anxious to maintain her *incognito*
when a coming storm is hanging in the air, are
only in the natural order of things, and I guarded
the secret of her literary assistance by every means
in my power.

'L. E. L.,' which reminds me of a Mrs. Thomson who was an intimate friend of hers also, and who has a claim on you, both by the force of novels and of historical writing. To return to Mrs. S. C. Hall,—her Irish tales (I am turning this pen round and round to find a writable side to it, and all in vain), her Irish tales have character and life, tenderness and softness—*not* power, and *not* passion—while her miscellaneous sketches in general are graceful and womanly, and the last in the most amiable sense.

"Lover you certainly should mention; and as to your 'five words,' you deserve to be impaled upon them yourself, if you give him no more. He is a powerful writer of Irish novels, and falls into the ranks after Banim,—with less passion than the latter, but more picturesque vivacity.

"You probably know his ballads, which have a certain singable beauty in them and a happy occasional fancifulness. His novels, however, all of which I have not read, are the stuff whereof his fame is made; and they are highly vital, and of great value in the sense of commenting on the national character.

"As to Lever, . . . I come to a stand. Ask Miss Mitford what she thinks of the 'Harry Lorrequers,' and she will tell you that the right royal 'Boz' is nothing 'at all at all' to the 'Lorrequers.' This is one of the thousand points on which she and I 'divide,' with no prospect of meeting again—for I *cannot read* Lever—honestly and without affectation, I *cannot.* She says the reason is, that she has more sympathies with men as men; has associated with them more closely as social men, and acquired the power of comprehending their social pleasures better than I, or women in general, have found it possible to do.*

"That is probably true; but it scarcely explains to me her admiration for Lorrequer (or Rollicker) Lever. Over and over again have I tried to read his book, and every time I came to the inference that he was a remarkably clever writer who was unreadable by me. Now it cannot be affectation—can it?—in a person who never pretends to 'lady-like delicacies' about the sort of book she reads. *I*, who read the old plays and the modern French romances (behind a screen—don't tell Mr. R——) cannot be hyper-super-over-particular; and I have read Balzac's 'Père Goriot,'

---

* Miss Mitford's father was a jovial, stick-at-nothing, fox-hunting squire of the three-bottle class.

and have *not* (could not) one of Lever's
novels. What the French call 'material
life' is the whole life he recognises.
That life is a jest, and a very loud one,
is his philosophy. The sense of Beauty
and Love he does not recognise at all,
except in a gross and conventional sense.
The chapters I have read of him make
my head ache as if I had been sitting
in the next room to an orgy—not an
orgy of fawns, O Orion! which even I
could feel the rapture of—but of gentle-
men-topers, with their low gentility and
hip-hip hurrah! and wine out of wine-
coolers. The headache does of course
prove the *power*, and that he is an exceedingly clever writer 'nobody *can*
deny;' but he is contracted and conventional, and unrefined in his line of
conventionalities; and I cannot believe
that he represents fairly even the social

and jovial side of men of much refine-
ment, or that, if he does, he should
represent them as he does, on all sides
thus social and jovial. No writer can
render human nature fully, who does
not render the inner and spiritual life
as well as the conventional and material
exterior of life. Is not this true? So
much for the Lorrequers.

"Not having read a single volume
through, and being of incompetent sympathies, my opinion is not certainly
worth much. I hear some of my brothers say sometimes, 'Oh, that Lever
is a capital fellow! better than "Boz;"'
and then I grow quite cross, and make
answer, 'Do put away those detestable
books of his,' or 'You don't deserve to
read "Boz."' 'Capital fellow,' though,
is just the criticism for him. He is *that*
—and no more, I think.

"Something more I wished to say to you, but cannot, perhaps could not, even if all this had not been written too lightly for a very earnest word to touch nearly in the sequence of it. But I must say this, if I have appeared to you lately—at any time, as I am afraid I must have done—deficient in feeling and sympathy and consideration—the appearance wronged me as much as. my hastiness has sometimes wronged *you*. You will understand, and *I* did not understand.

"May God bless you, dear Mr. Horne. I am glad that the labour is near at an end, and that you are going out of town to finish. 'To finish' makes an agreeable idea. Ever truly yours,

"E. B. B."

END OF VOL I.

www.ingramcontent.com/pod-product-compliance
Lightning Source LLC
Chambersburg PA
CBHW021842070726
47496CB00022B/1802